TYLER PYLE

Bone Runes

Arcane Rebirth

CLARKY PUBLICATION

Contents

Dedication

Dear Mom and Dad,
This is dedicated to you. Through all the hardship and all the struggle we have faced as a family, I am thankful you are my parents. While it wasn't always easy, I wouldn't change it for the world.
From all the notebooks of stories I've filled since I was a child, to the sleepless nights in prayer for you two, I am thankful to call you my mom and dad. You two have raised me, taught me, and molded me into being able to love, hope, and remember the possibilities of what God can do, even in the most troublesome times.
If I had to do it all over, I would, just to have you two as you are now. Thank you for the love and support over the course of my life.
Love,
Your Son.

Color Index

RED (Fire, Heat, Destruction)

Crimson Red – Extreme heat, firestorm magic, combustion
   Blood Red – Life-burning flames, consuming both enemy and user
   Scarlet Red – Magma and molten rock manipulation
   Dark Red – Demonic fire, unholy flames that devour souls
   Bright Red – Pure flame, fastest fire magic
Hybrid Red
   Red + Pink = Inferno Fist → Fire-infused punches with burning impacts
   Red + Gray = Firestorm Wind → Creates swirling vortexes of flame
   Red + Black = Hellfire → Unholy, soul-burning flames
BLUE (Water, Ice, Pressure)
   Sky Blue – Mist and steam magic
   Deep Ocean Blue – Water pressure control, deep-sea strength
   Icy Blue – Cryomancy (Ice magic, frost-based attacks)
   Dark Blue – Water compression and slicing techniques
Hybrid Blue
   Blue + Pink = Tidal Force → Shockwave punches and fluid combat movements
   Blue + Yellow = Storm Surge → Water-based electricity

Blue + White = Holy Water → Purification and healing

GREEN (Nature, Growth, Poison, Life Magic)

Bright Green – Healing and plant growth

Dark Forest Green – Poisonous vines and toxic spores

Lime Green – Acid magic, corrosive spells

Hybrid Green

Green + Pink = Nature Titan → Becomes a plant-powered warrior, growing in strength

Green + Brown = Earth Guardian → Controls both plants and stone

Green + Blue = Swamp Sorcery → Uses water-based poison magic

BROWN (Earth, Metal, Stone, Gravity)

Light Brown – Sand and shifting terrain

Dark Brown – Stone and rock magic

Golden Brown – Metal manipulation, armor creation

Hybrid Brown

Brown + Pink = Titan's Might → Stone-powered muscle, unbreakable defense

Brown + Black = Abyssal Earth → Shadow-infused land control

Brown + Green = Nature Titan → Stone and plant-based fusion attacks

YELLOW (Energy, Speed, Time Magic)

Bright Yellow – Super speed, agility boosts

Golden Yellow – Time magic, time-slowing abilities (Illegal)

Static Yellow – Electric-based attacks

Hybrid Yellow

Yellow + Pink = Lightning Charge → Supercharged muscle and reflex speed

Yellow + Red = Plasma Surge → Fire-infused electrical attacks

Yellow + Purple = Chrono Break → Temporal attacks, time

acceleration

GRAY (Wind, Air, Storms)

Light Gray – Soft wind, breeze magic

Storm Gray – Hurricane winds, thunderstorm generation

Smoky Gray – Gas and airborne toxins

Hybrid Gray

Gray + Pink = Wind Walker → Airborne combat, gravity-reduced movement

Gray + Yellow = Lightning Storm → Storm magic combining wind and electricity

Gray + Blue = Tsunami Winds → Wind-powered tidal waves

PURPLE (Illusions, Space, Forbidden Magic)

Soft Purple – Mind manipulation, illusion-based magic

Dark Purple – Space and void-based magic (Illegal)

Astral Violet – Dimensional warping

Hybrid Purple

Purple + Pink = Warping Crush → Can send physical attacks through dimensions

Purple + Black = Shadow Rift → Creates portals into darkness

Purple + Yellow = Chrono-Void → Merges time and space magic for short time jumps

BLACK (Shadow, Darkness, Void, Necromancy)

Deep Black – Manipulates shadows and darkness

Void Black – Can remove things from existence (Illegal)

Hybrid Black

Black + Pink = Phantom Force → Strength-based shadow attacks, can phase through strikes

Black + Brown = Abyssal Earth → Controls shadow-infused stone

Black + Purple = Shadow Rift → Travel through voids

WHITE (Light, Holy, Purification)

Bright White – Holy light, cleansing magic

Silver White – Purification and divine attacks

Hybrid White

White + Pink = Angel's Strength → Heavenly strength that purifies evil on impact

White + Black = Balance Magic → The rarest magic, combining light and darkness

White + Purple = Divine Space → Holy teleportation

PINK (Power, Strength, Enhancement)

Magenta Pink – Aura-based combat, energy-infused attacks

Hot Pink – Berserker state, grants temporary invulnerability but drains the user

Light Pastel Pink – Compression-based strength, lifting massive objects

Dark Crimson Rose – Forbidden strength, capable of breaking human limits

Hybrid Pink

Pink + Yellow = Lightning Charge → Super-speed strength enhancement

Pink + Red = Inferno Fist → Fire-enhanced martial arts

Pink + Gray = Wind Walker → Airborne melee combat

Forbidden Magic (Illegal and Deadly)

Chrono-Void (Dark Purple + Golden Yellow) → Controls both space and time, breaking reality

Phoenix Flames (Blood Red + Holy White) → Fire that burns away fate itself

Abyssal Destruction (Void Black + Red) → Creates black holes that erase anything

God's Wrath (Dark Crimson Rose + Any Color) → Strength that surpasses mortal limits, but risks burning out life force

1

BLACKWOOD ACADEMY

There are moments in life that define your very existence. For some, it's how they die, going out in a glorious final "hurrah." For others, it's the quiet legacy of raising a family, planting the seeds of a new generation that might leave an even greater mark.

For Thomas, it was the moment the bullies pushed him just a little too far.

Thomas Aldric was a 14-year-old boy preparing to start his first year of high school. His most notable feature was the streaks of white that ran through his bangs, contrasting against the auburn hair that hung flat over his forehead. His eyes were a matching auburn with a glimmer that often went unnoticed. By all accounts, Thomas was considered "average", just another kid. Except, he lived in an orphanage.

Like many kids, Thomas was bullied. Most of it was mild: name-calling and teasing about his looks or personality. But sometimes it cuts deeper, jabs at his self-worth, cruel remarks about being passed around the foster system like a hot potato.

Families rarely kept him long. Emotional flare-ups seemed to follow him, triggered simply by his presence. It was like there was an aura around him, heavy, unshakable, and beyond his control.

The most recent incident happened six months ago. The family had been foster parents for quite some time—one of the most respected in the system, having taken in hundreds of children over the past 20 years. But they weren't as they had been described. The father was quieter than expected and seemed irritated whenever he made eye contact with Thomas.

Thomas could never figure out why.

One day, he accidentally knocked over a glass of water at the table. The father exploded, shouting without restraint. His temper snapped. That night, Thomas was taken back to the orphanage with little to no explanation.

A few days later, the family contacted the orphanage to apologize. Like many before them, they claimed not to understand what had come over them. They described it as a slow-burning rage that built up inside.

Regardless, Thomas was back at the orphanage—and they never tried to take him in again.

He used to dream of finding a forever family. But the older he got, the less likely it seemed. Older kids were rarely adopted, and without siblings, his chances felt even slimmer.

"Thomas? Earth to Thomas."

A woman's voice cut through the haze, and Thomas blinked back to awareness. He looked up, meeting the warm gaze of the woman seated in front of him. The quiet tick of a wall clock filled the room. He sat sunken into a memory foam couch, fingers digging into the cushions.

Across from him sat a young brunette woman with tan skin

and glasses, smiling gently. She held a clipboard with a pencil clipped to it. When Thomas met her brown eyes, he tensed and blushed.

"Thomas, hon, it's okay," she said softly.

Still, the tightness in his chest didn't ease.

"Right. I'm sorry. What was the question again, Ms. Riley?" His words came out tentative, embarrassment creeping over him.

"No, no, it's fine, sweetheart. I was just asking if the dreams have stopped."

Her voice was kind and calm, but her reassurance didn't reach him. His eyes flicked away, either because of her beauty or because of the secret he was too scared to tell.

"No... my dreams stopped," he said.

It was a lie. One that only hurt him more. She scribbled on the clipboard—harsh, scratchy sounds that felt like needles in his ears. Her tentative smile, her happiness—it was all because of his lie.

His throat tightened. His mind buzzed, but the thoughts were scrambled, unreadable. Just the weight of the lie, pressing down.

"Good! Then the medicine's working!" Her face lit up with joy.

She was one of the few people who seemed to care. But the medication wasn't working. His body didn't respond to it; it was like he was immune.

Still, he couldn't bring himself to tell her the truth.

The nightmares were getting worse. They always ended the same way: bloodshed and collapse. The world crumbling in on itself.

He could never remember all the details, but the feelings

lingered. The scent of roses, the stench of burned flesh. He always woke up crying, knees buried in imagined rubble.

He'd reach instinctively to his chest pocket as if expecting to find something that was never there. Something always felt missing.

"How's your head? Still getting headaches?"

"On occasion."

"When your routine is disrupted?"

Thomas hesitated, then nodded.

They said he had autism, high functioning, whatever that meant, and also diagnosed him with paranoid schizophrenia. Shadows. Whispers. Voices. They called them symptoms.

But to Thomas, they felt at home, like someone was watching over him as a parent might.

"What about the outbursts?"

"It's been a week since I snapped."

"The school board said you flipped a desk. Is that true?"

Thomas froze. He didn't remember doing that, but she was right. The desk flipped. Everyone stared. The pressure in his head, the pounding behind his eyes.

One of the kids started harassing him—he couldn't even remember what it was about. But he remembered the swelling in his stomach, the tightness in his chest, and how his breathing grew heavy.

His ears rang, filling his head with a sharp, torturous pain— like a dog whistle drilling straight through.

Then he snapped. He raised a finger to speak, but instead, the desk flew off his lap and crashed to the ground.

Had he flipped it? He asked himself that a lot. Maybe he did. Maybe it caught on his button-up. Thomas wasn't sure.

He nodded slowly. What else could he say?

Their time was up. Relief softened his shoulders as he stood and slipped out the door, back into the towering halls of the private school.

He walked quickly, his flannel jacket draped over his uniform, eyes locked on the floor. He didn't dare look at anyone.

All he wanted was to get to his next class and finish the day without falling apart.

He had tried to avoid summer school. His grades were passable, but poor attendance and missing assignments backed him into a corner, landing him at Blackwood Academy for the summer. The prestigious hellhole served as a PR move for the orphanage more than anything else. Its insignia, a black pine tree encircled by a thin white stripe, sat proudly on every uniform. And the motto? *"The Unseen Shall Lead."* Thomas hated it. It made him feel like he was being groomed for a secret society.

Thomas stood in silence, staring at the motto printed on the banner hanging in the hallway. His eyes flicked over the words again and again, letting them sink in. Around him, kids moved through the corridor—heels clicking against the tile, voices rising and fading.

When he finally looked away, his chest felt tight again.

Students passed him, whispering. Was it about him?

He wondered how it couldn't be.

He reached up and touched the white streak in the bangs of his hair, letting out a quiet sigh. Then, slowly, he started walking again—blending back into the routine.

The teachers were tolerable. The students? Not so much. They were a chaotic mix of elites, orphans, and regular kids, some of whom mysteriously vanished right before the school year began. The official word was always "transfer," but the rumors and ghost stories said otherwise.

The hallways gleamed with trophies and accolades, show-casing MVPs across medicine, science, sports, you name it. Students pushed hard to succeed. The girls were book-smart, the boys athletic. At the bottom? Dante is a loudmouthed bully who dumps all his misery on Thomas.

Religious studies was Thomas' last class of the day. It was laid-back, tolerable, and taught by someone who didn't care enough to yell. Castel, a student aid from a local college, made it even more bearable.

"Well, there's the old man," Castel said, walking in.

"Hello, Castel," Thomas muttered, trying to stay under the radar. Castel was tall, maybe eighteen, with slick black hair and enough piercings to set off metal detectors. He had that rebellious charm, converse shoes, skinny jeans, dog tags and a button-up shirt tucked in like he was trying *just enough*.

For reasons Thomas didn't understand, Castel had gravitated toward him on day one. Maybe he saw a loner. Maybe he just liked helping out. Either way, Castel made the days easier.

"What did you eat today? I had chicken strips, extra crunchy, dipped in black peppered ranch, with seasoned fries. *Delicioso!*" Castel spun a chair backward and plopped down with flair.

"I had PB&J," Thomas smirked. "Also *delicioso*."

Castel grinned. "Next time, my treat. We'll eat real food. Deal?"

Thomas chuckled, catching a few glances from classmates. "Fine, we'll eat."

Castel was busy—Thomas knew that all too well. Still, every now and then, they managed to meet up. Castel usually treated him to a burger and fries, depending on what they were in the mood for.

Sometimes, he'd show up with food and share it without saying much. Thomas had asked why a few times, but Castel always gave the same answer:

"Ah, you know. Why not."

It wasn't much of an explanation, and even with summer school almost over, Thomas still couldn't get more out of him.

A ruler tapped the desk. Castel stood and returned the chair to its place, taking a seat up front as the teacher began.

Religious studies weren't boring. In fact, Thomas found them fascinating. Norse mythology, runes, gods, and old magic all pulled him in. He could imagine being there, feeling the cold air and hearing battle cries echo across snow-covered fields.

Today's topic was the Algernon, an ancient Viking group said to have been blessed by the gods with extraordinary abilities passed down through royal blood. They'd vanished from history, assimilated or erased. No one knew for sure.

Their belief? That they were pure—gifted with abilities from the Gods. They claimed to have magic granted to them, giving them access to a kind of magical weave. It supposedly enhanced their abilities, and in some cases, gave them control over the elements.

Thomas thought the idea was cool, but way too good to be true.

Still, that didn't stop him from daydreaming about being one of them—a Viking with fireballs, like in an RPG. He pictured the ocean breeze in his hair as they sailed the seas... minus all the pillaging, of course.

While most students dozed, Thomas sat mesmerized. The bell rang. He hadn't even noticed the time fly. He packed up slowly, watching Castel chat with the teacher like old friends. Thomas figured he'd catch him later and began walking the halls alone. The rhythm of his footsteps grounded him, helping to dull the restless fire in his head.

Outside, the sun hit his skin like a warm hand. He closed his eyes, brief serenity until a carton of milk smashed against his head. Milk was sprayed everywhere.

It was chunky, and the smell hit him hard—instantly making Thomas's stomach turn. The liquid was already soaking into his clothes. If he hadn't seen the carton lying on the ground in front of him, he might've thought someone had nailed him with cottage cheese.

The thought alone made him want to throw up.

"Check it out, it's Thoe," Dante jeered.

Thomas stayed silent. He knew fighting would get him nowhere, so he kept walking. Dante and his goons followed, taunting him with jabs about his looks, his build, and his unknown family.

As they passed the gates, Dante pushed him hard. Thomas stumbled, his knees scraping the sidewalk. "You're gonna be one of those missing kids," Dante sneered.

Thomas didn't respond.

"Do something!" Dante shoved him again, harder. Thomas fell again. His patience was thinning.

Then, fingers tangled in his hair.

Dante dragged him into a nearby alley. Thomas had taken beatings before, but something about this felt... off. He tried to resist, but Dante hurled him against the wall. His lungs emptied with a painful wheeze.

The alleyway walls felt like they were closing in, his vision narrowing with them. Dante was too close—Thomas could smell the burger he'd had for lunch.

His lungs couldn't get enough air. Sweat rolled down his palms. His legs felt like jelly.

He needed to get out. Now.

"We're about to be high schoolers," Dante growled. "And you're gonna help me get straight A's. Make my GPA shine. Maybe, just maybe, I'll let you be my assistant someday."

Thomas stared at him.

Dante's usual routine shifted. He sent his lackeys away. Just the two of them now. The air felt heavier. A bad omen.

Dante's fist slammed into the wall beside Thomas's head. "Do we have a deal?"

On any other day, Thomas might have said yes. But something inside cracked.

"Eat dicks," he spat.

Dante's punch came fast, landing on his cheek. Thomas reeled.

"Say that again," Dante hissed.

Thomas couldn't stop himself. "Eat. Dic-"

A punch to the gut cut him off. Vomit hit the concrete. His lunch was smeared on the ground.

Then... something inside snapped.

Staggering forward, Thomas swung. He missed, but something else didn't.

The world around them flickered for a split second like reality glitched.

The hairs on his arms stood up. Everything around him felt... off, like the world had shifted out of place.

A low buzzing filled the air. Dante's body twisted unnaturally, like he was frozen mid-movement—glitched.

It was as if the world itself was a computer simulation, and someone had just tripped a bug in the code.

A sickening squelch echoed through the air, like a water balloon bursting.

Thomas braced for retaliation, expecting Dante to strike back after his missed punch. But something was wrong.

Blood trickled from Dante's eyes, ears, nose, and mouth. His skin was pale, and his pupils had lost all focus. Without a sound, he fell backward and hit the ground with a thud.

Thomas froze.

He stared at the boy who had bullied him for so long, now unmoving on the pavement. Panic took hold. He dropped to his knees and grabbed Dante's shoulders, his own body trembling, swelling with a strange pressure like it was filling with liquid.

"D-Dante," he stammered.

His fingers pressed against Dante's neck. No pulse. The skin was cold.

A frantic scream tore from Thomas' throat as he staggered back. Then he turned and bolted.

It was self-defense! All I did was try to punch him! I didn't do it. He had a heart attack from being fat!

Thoughts slammed through his mind, overlapping and suffocating, but underneath it all, there was... silence. For the first time in forever, the noise in his brain was gone.

Then came the nausea.

He bent over and vomited, bile splashing onto the alley floor. His hands clutched his stomach, his whole body shaking from the flood of adrenaline and horror. He dragged himself forward, crawling before finally pushing to his feet.

And then, he ran.

His legs moved like they had minds of their own, carrying him with the speed of an athlete. Somehow, in all the terror, his mind felt more precise and sharper. His thoughts raced, but, for once, they made sense.

He rounded the corner and spotted the orphanage in the distance.

Should he hide? Turn himself in?

Would they try him as an adult? Was his life over?

The clarity didn't make the answers easier. If anything, the thoughts were clearer but cruel. Still, Thomas had only one plan: get back to his room and figure out what to do next.

2

INSANITY OR REALITY

Thomas arrived at the orphanage not long after everything happened. Most of the staff didn't bother him, and while they were kind enough, they'd long stopped hoping he'd be adopted. At fourteen, he was too old in their eyes. In four years, he'd age out of the system and be on his own. Their focus had shifted to simply getting him through high school. After that, he'd be left to figure out the rest on his own.

There was silence. A few workers passed by, avoiding eye contact. Most were too busy to say anything to him.

They had other kids to look after. They didn't have time for him.

One unexpected perk of being given up on was privacy. He had his bedroom now, and they let him do whatever he wanted with it. With a racing heart, he slipped through the large double doors of the orphanage, his pace quickening. His face had gone pale. Dante's image still followed him, burned into his mind. That same bloated, lifeless version of Dante lingering in the shadows of the hallway haunted him. His breath hitched.

The hallway where he stood was lined with posters. Most were adoption encouragements—smiling families, bright slogans, and photos of kids who had found their forever homes.

Some of the pictures and pamphlets were curled at the edges, worn from being flipped through again and again by visitors.

He could hear the lounge—the TV blaring in the background—but no one paid him any attention. He was like a ghost on the wall, a necessary evil.

They ignored him, yet he was the one keeping the younger kids in check. He watched over them, helped them with math and science, even read them books at night to help them sleep.

Everyone may have acted like he wasn't there, but they couldn't manage without him.

"Thomas! Thomas! How was your day?"

Thomas flinched at the sudden voice. It was Samuel, a ten-year-old who'd taken to following him around.

Samuel was harmless. He had short brown hair and golden eyes, and he was still full of innocence. Thomas figured he'd be adopted soon. The boy was new, recently orphaned after a car accident took his parents.

Thomas forced a weak smile, his eyes still wide with lingering fear. He ruffled Samuel's hair then gently pushed his head away to avoid eye contact. He couldn't bear to look into his innocent eyes—they only made the ache in his chest worse.

His hands trembled against Samuel's head, his whole body aching with it.

"G-Good, kid. I... I've got a lot of homework to do."

It was a lie. He'd forgotten it was summer school, and there was never any homework, just quizzes done in class. Thankfully, Samuel didn't question it and watched as Thomas continued down the hall. But Samuel's voice echoed down the hallway before he could.

"Don't forget, I have an adoption appointment coming up! I'm going to have a forever home!"

His words were full of life and hope—things Thomas had lost a lifetime ago.

He was happy for Samuel. He just wished he knew what that felt like.

The foyer buzzed with activity. Other kids ate snacks and drank water, chatting in small groups. Thomas slipped past them, avoiding eye contact, trying not to be seen.

"Dante was following Thomas again," someone whispered.

It was a classmate talking to a girl who didn't have to attend summer school.

"No way. Again?" she frowned. "You think that's why he's late? Maybe he and Dante got into trouble."

Thomas didn't stick around to hear more. He darted to the stairwell, dodging a group of younger kids running past, then hurried up to the second floor. In his room, he shut the door and locked it.

Only then did the adrenaline fade, and the weight of every-thing crashed down.

Tears ran down his cheeks as he gripped the doorframe. Gasping and sobbing, he stumbled back and collapsed to the floor, hugging his knees. His thoughts were blank, his brain silent. He couldn't even blink, and his eyes stung from dryness as a breeze slid across them.

The floor was dusty—he hadn't swept in a while. Old, torn posters clung to the walls, and clothes were scattered every-where from the laundry he hadn't gotten to.

Lately, he'd been focused on getting the younger kids' laundry done at night while everyone else got ready for bed.

The smell of Dante still clung to his nose—how could it not, when the figure of Dante lingered in the corner of his eye the entire time?

He clawed at the floorboards, but his nails weren't long enough to do anything. He dry heaved, desperate to ease the churn in his stomach, but nothing came up.

His forehead pressed against the floor, the scent of dust and dirt barely masking the smell of Dante.

Then, suddenly, he blinked, and the sun was gone.

He lay limp on the floor, sweat dripping from his forehead. Had he fallen asleep... or passed out?

Pushing himself up, he grabbed the clock nearby. **2:00 AM.**

He'd been out cold for hours.

His head swam, sweat rolling down his face as he lifted himself off the floor.

He clutched his stomach—it growled, but the hunger felt more like pain. The room around him was dark, and his body ached like he'd been hit by a truck.

Slowly, he pushed himself up. Turning toward the window, his gaze fell on the distant town where Dante's body would be. Had they found it yet? Were his parents still searching? Maybe the police were testing the vomit Thomas left behind.

A wave of dread tightened around his chest. He couldn't breathe.

He turned back, grabbed his bag, and began stuffing clothes into it. He didn't own much, so packing was easy.

I'll leave. Just disappear. No one will miss me. I'm nobody, he told himself.

He paused at the window, backpack slung over his shoulders. He stared out at the path leading away from the orphanage. The world beyond was dim, save for the flickering of distant streetlights.

He climbed out and gripped the vines that clung to the building's outer walls, slowly lowering himself down, rough gray bricks beneath them. The orphanage had stood since the 1940s, quietly serving its purpose ever since.

Most of the kids came from the big city an hour away—it offered a bit of calm in otherwise dark circumstances.

The climb felt endless, though maybe that was just the noise in his head. Dante's voice echoed in his mind, relentless, reminding him of what he'd done.

Once on the ground, he began walking, eyes on the pavement. He couldn't bring himself to look up. The night always made things worse. His eyes felt like they watched him from the shadows, and whispers crept in.

Schizophrenia always hits harder at night.

The farther he walked, the stronger the presence felt. It was like something was breathing down his neck.

Finally, he reached the fork of three paths.

To the right: the school.

To the left: the road out of town.

Straight ahead: the town center.

Leaving town wasn't an option. The road led to nowhere, just woods and wildlife. He'd starve, or worse.

Straight ahead led deeper into town. He could hide in alleys, maybe sleep in the park's tunnels. But there'd be people, passersby. And if anyone got suspicious, the whole town would be after him.

School was the best option. It had a forest behind it. He could sneak in at sunrise when the janitors opened the doors, grab food from his locker, and then hide out in the woods. He could wait a week, then raid the garden club's vegetables when they were ripe. But could he survive that long?

He clicked his tongue in frustration, then adjusted his backpack and started toward the school.

The summer breeze nipped at his arms, sending goosebumps up his skin. His headache worsened the closer he got. As he neared the gate, he tossed his bag over, climbed up, and dropped down with a thud, his backpack cushioning the fall.

Groaning, he stood, slung the bag over his shoulder, and moved toward the woods.

Almost there.

Then, a hand gripped his shoulder.

Thomas froze, the color draining from his face. The pain in his head spiked like something screamed in his ears. The pressure rang through his skull.

He turned slowly and locked eyes with Castel.

That familiar face, and suddenly, the weight of guilt crushed him. He felt like he'd betrayed something sacred.

"What's wrong? Why are you here so early?" Castel asked, brows furrowed with concern.

Thomas opened his mouth to speak, but nothing came out. The words caught in his throat.

I was exploring the woods.

I wanted to bask in the moonlight.

But neither would come.

"I killed Dante," the words burst out, a messy mix of guilt, relief, and panic. Tears followed. "I don't know how. I just tried to punch him!"

Thomas collapsed, body trembling, but Castel caught him, steadying him with a firm grip.

"Hey, Woah now. Calm down," Castel said, voice confused but steady. "Let's figure this out."

A long, drawn-out silence followed, broken only by Thomas's quiet weeping.

With a soft breath, Castel placed a hand on his shoulder. He couldn't leave him like this—not in the state he was in.

He glanced around, trying to figure out the best way to handle it.

Sitting in the principal's office, Thomas held a cup of tea Castel had made for him. It was some kind of herbal remedy, hot and oddly reminiscent of a strawberry pastry. The warmth settled into him, relaxing his body and mind. Despite having been awake since 2 a.m., the tea made him feel as if he'd had a full night's sleep. The clock now read 7 a.m. Sunlight streamed through the windows as students began arriving for the final Friday of summer school.

The scent of tea lingered in the air. It tasted as good as it smelled, but the warmth did nothing to keep what happened from bringing the uneasiness to his stomach.

The ticking clock sounded like a drumbeat in his ears, each tick counting down the seconds until his sentence—until his downfall.

It was too much. He wanted to stand, leap out the window, and follow through with his escape plan. But it was too late.

They knew. He knew. And soon, the world would know what he had done.

His knee bounced with restless energy. His stomach felt like a balloon, tight and ready to burst.

Maybe this is what Dante felt in his final moments.

Thomas sat silently, listening to the faint voices outside and the steady ticking of the clock. His headache had vanished shortly after he began drinking the tea. The whispers and shadows were gone, too. He slowly scanned the room, taking in the pictures, shelves lined with awards, and plaques the principal had earned over the years.

A murmur outside the door made him tense.

"Any signs of Dante?" asked a voice Ms. Riley's, he thought.

Guilt tightened in his chest. He had failed her. He had failed Castel. He would never see his only friend again. And after what he had done, there was no future left for him. The thoughts weighed heavy on his brain, but they still didn't compare to the moment he had actually done it.

They won't find him. His corpse is in an alleyway. The words looped in his mind, relentless.

Then, silence.

The door creaked open. The principal stepped in.

He was an older man with salt-and-pepper hair and a neatly trimmed goatee. Thomas looked away, trying to swallow the lump in his throat. The man's presence filled the room tall, broad, dressed in a sharp grey suit. He took care of himself, his athletic frame still visible beneath the fabric.

Thomas had never had a problem with him. He was intim-idating, sure, but fair. A stand-up guy who had come to this academy with the hope of helping all kinds of students.

"Thomas, can you tell me what happened? In detail," the principal asked. His name was James, but Thomas couldn't remember it right then. It had slipped from his mind.

"Dante was bullying me... I went to punch him, but I thought

I missed. Instead, he just... started bleeding from all his face holes. His nose, ears, mouth, everything. Then he swelled up like a balloon and hit the ground."

The words rushed out of him. Fast. Nervous. His stomach twisted. If there had been anything in it besides tea, he might've thrown up.

James gave a small wave toward the door.

It opened.

And stepped Dante.

Chubby. Quiet. Alive.

Thomas froze. Dante's eyes locked on him, filled with a simmering rage that promised fists after school. But Thomas wasn't focused on that.

The world froze again.

Dante's stupid, bloated face stared at him.

Everything felt cold. Voices rushed through Thomas's head—disbelief, doubt, the creeping fear that maybe he was losing his mind, even though he knew exactly what he had seen.

His eyes darted to James, Ms. Riley, and Castel. They were all staring at him, their faces tight with worry and confusion.

The clock had stopped ticking. The tea had lost its steam.

And yet, he still saw Dante's corpse—standing right next to Dante. Two sets of eyes. Both locked on him.

Both cutting straight through him.

His body shot backward, tipping over the chair and sending the glass cup flying. It shattered across the floor. He stumbled back, pale as a ghost.

"No. No, no! He was dead! He was lying there dead!" Thomas screamed, eyes wide, voice cracking. Ms. Riley and Castle appeared in the doorway, their faces etched with worry as if watching someone unravel.

James raised a hand and turned to Dante.

"Dante, please. Tell us what you saw."

Dante hesitated, then cleared his throat. His eyes darted away.

"We… We were in an alley. Alone. You swung at me. I closed my eyes to brace for it, and when I opened them, you were gone."

It didn't make sense. None of it made sense.

The room felt unreal like it was bending and shifting. Thomas felt sick. He was detached as if he were floating above his own body, watching this unfold from a distance.

He opened his mouth. Nothing came out. Just a dry rasp.

Ms. Riley gently guided Dante out and turned back with a frown.

"Maybe… we should adjust his medication. Thomas, you've been taking it, haven't you?"

He hadn't. He wouldn't. But before he could respond, James cut in.

"Ms. Riley, I need to speak with Thomas alone, and since Castel found him, I'd like him to stay, too."

Ms. Riley hesitated, glancing at Thomas like she might never see him again. The door clicked shut behind her.

Castel stepped in, uprighted the chair, and then crouched to collect the shattered pieces of glass and mop up the spilled tea. When he finished, he sat beside Thomas and gently guided him back into the chair.

Thomas stayed quiet. His mind raced. Everything felt like a trap.

Maybe I am crazy, he thought, watching James speak but hearing nothing.

Castel was talking, too. Still, no sound.

Thomas pressed his palms to his ears, trying to force sound back into them. A dull ache began to build behind his temples, and his breath quickened.

Why can't I hear anything?

Suddenly, the world snapped back into place. The clock ticked, James cleared his throat, and Castel's chair squeaked.

"Thomas," James said, "we think you're special."

Castel leaned on one elbow, overseeing him.

"We want to take you to a new school. One Castel attends. They send us advisors every year to recruit students with extraordinary gifts like yours."

Before he could finish, Thomas interrupted.

"Crazy people," he muttered, bitter. "You recruit nut jobs. That's where all the kids go when they vanish because you think they're insane?"

James and Castel fell silent for a moment.

"It's not like that," Castel said gently. "I've been going for over a year. The school can help you. The migraines, the pressure in your head, the paranoia, everything. They understand."

Thomas stared at him. How did he know about that? He hadn't told him. Ms. Riley, maybe? But he trusted her. Didn't he?

His thoughts spiraled, but Castel's sincerity grounded him. Slowly, the gears in his mind clicked into place.

He rubbed his palms against his jeans and stared at the floor.

What would Ms. Riley think if he left the school to follow Castel into a new world?

And Samuel—would he be okay without him? What would

happen to the orphanage? What would happen to *him*?

The soft ticking of the clock returned, steady and quiet. The eyes were still on him.

His thoughts began to fog.

At least there was one bright side—no more Dante. He couldn't face him again. Couldn't handle seeing a corpse alive and walking around.

He wouldn't. He *refused* to.

"Fine," he whispered.

It was all too much. The last twelve hours had been a nightmare.

He just wanted to sleep.

3

YOU, ME, AND BRODY

The day was far from normal for Thomas. His usual tics and habits flared up, his tongue clicked more rapidly, his scratching more frequent, and most of all, the pressure in his skull pulsed like a ticking clock. But one thing had changed: the eerie eyes in the shadows were gone. That ever-present gaze, the sense of being watched, vanished. In its absence, he felt strangely alone, as if he'd lost something important. Yet, deep down, it reassured him that maybe, just maybe, the path he'd chosen was the right one.

He was excused from the final day of summer school. Castel had walked him back to the orphanage in near silence. Thomas had a million questions, but somehow, he knew none would be answered, at least not yet. Whatever answers there were, they'd be waiting at the school.

The orphanage had already been informed of his acceptance before he even stepped off school grounds. When the double doors opened, he was met with a wave of excited screams that left him stunned.

Thomas had spent his whole life in that building. He never knew his parents. As a baby, he'd been left on the doorstep with nothing but a small blanket long since passed on to another child, not out of neglect but by his own choice. If his parents didn't want him, he didn't want to hold on to anything of theirs.

Despite the distance the workers now kept, they were the only family he'd ever known. He didn't cause trouble. The real reason for his tardiness and missed school days was simple: he stayed behind to care for the sick kids. If he'd been the troublemaker everyone assumed, he would've met James much earlier.

It was true Thomas struggled with his mental health. Ms. Riley had prescribed him antidepressants, anxiety meds, and even a small blue pill to suppress his nightmares. None of them worked. The weight of his life pressed down relentlessly. He often felt like he was teetering on the edge, the thought of ending it all lurking in the back of his mind. He had no real hope for the future.

And yet, standing in the foyer, surrounded by banners and cheers from the only people who'd ever known him, he felt something shift. There was pressure in his chest, heavy with guilt and sorrow. He was leaving them all behind for a new life at a mysterious academy.

The orphanage had splurged on cake and snacks. Kids squealed and dashed around, high on sugar. Thomas felt bad for the staff who'd have to wrangle them into bed later. Castel was off answering questions about the school, but his answers were vague and evasive—Thomas barely listened. Something about it all felt deliberately hidden. The image of bloated, lifeless Dante flashed in his memory. He still believed what he saw was real.

Holding a slice of double fudge chocolate cake, he stared at it for a long moment. Was this all a dream? Had he finally snapped? Was this the break from reality he'd feared? Shaking the thought away, he shoved the moist cake into his mouth. Fresh cake only ever meant one thing: someone had been adopted. And this was the closest Thomas would get to that.

Castel and James had only shared the basics: the academy was private, four years long, room and board included, and it was near the ocean. *Loony bin*, Thomas had thought. Maybe it still was. But what did he have left to lose? All he wanted was to feel normal.

"Can you believe he was chosen for the academy?"

"Pretty strange, if you ask me."

The voices came from two classmates, the same ones whispering about Dante the day before. They were always together, like siblings glued at the hip.

"I bet it's a cult," the girl giggled.

"Just like the other kids during the summer," the boy added with a snort. "He's being shipped off to be sacrificed."

Their laughter trailed behind him as he sighed, set his cake down, and slipped away upstairs. The party had spread throughout the orphanage now. One kid was already passed out from the sugar crash.

In his room, he placed an old leather suitcase on the bed and started packing. He had little, just a few flannel shirts, a couple of undershirts, and two pairs of jeans. Since his school uniforms weren't needed, there wasn't much left to bring.

He glanced around the room at old scraps, worn toys, and torn posters he'd scavenged over the years. None of it meant much anymore.

"Thomas..." a small voice called out.

His ears perked. He turned to see little Samuel standing in the doorway, eyes red and face pale.

"Oh, hey, Sam. What's up?" he asked gently.

Samuel broke into tears.

Thomas knelt, arms open wide. Samuel launched into his embrace, sobbing uncontrollably. "I'm going to miss you," Thomas said softly. Samuel clung to him tighter, his words lost in gasping sobs.

Thomas let him cry. He rubbed Samuel's back gently until the boy started to calm down.

"Hey," Thomas said, wiping a tear from the boy's cheek, "I don't know what this school is like, but I promise to write to you. At least once a month, okay?"

Samuel nodded through stuttering breaths.

"I'll remind him too, Sport," Castel said from the doorway, leaning casually with a gentle smile and a reassuring wink.

Samuel couldn't respond; his heart was aching. He didn't know how to process it.

"Listen, buddy," Thomas said, cupping Samuel's cheek. "With me gone, I need you to be the protector of the orphanage, alright? If kids get sick, help the housekeepers. Help the adults watch the other kids. And most importantly, make friends. Work hard, and do your best to get adopted. Deal?"

Samuel pressed his face into Thomas's chest again, tears soaking the flannel jacket.

"I will, Thomas. I promise," he cried.

Thomas smiled, rubbing his back one last time. Afterward, he finished packing, leaving one of his flannels behind for Samuel, and headed out with Castel.

The orphanage had been his home. While the academy still felt like a one-way trip to a loony bin, he hoped he'd still be able to write Samuel from behind padded walls.

"Why are we going back to the academy, Castel?" Thomas asked quietly.

Castel didn't answer right away. Lost in thought? His eyes flicked to Thomas, and a small smile appeared.

"Oh, we're going through the forest to get there."

He said it like it was perfectly normal, but for Thomas, the words landed like a punch. He remembered the rumor he'd overheard about a secret underground tunnel beneath the forest that led to a cult's sacrificial chamber.

That memory haunted him.

Great. I'm gonna be sacrificed, Thomas thought. He wasn't sure what was worse, that thought or the fact that he was still willingly following Castel toward the trees.

"Well, make it painless, please," Thomas muttered.

Castel blinked in confusion, opening his mouth to respond, but Thomas cut him off.

"Seriously though, why the forest behind the school?" he asked again.

It was a fair question. From everything the students knew, that forest was fenced off with a tall brick wall. No one was supposed to go in or out.

After reaching the academy, they veered onto a narrow path that wound around the building, on the same path Thomas had once been caught wandering down by Castel.

"Well, let me ask you something, Thomas," Castel began, his tone casual. "Do you believe there's more to this world than meets the eye?"

The question struck Thomas as absurd. To him, the world had always seemed plain, logical, and predictable. He often wondered about life's meaning, whether a higher power existed, or if humanity was just clinging to a rock spinning through space by accident.

"I think it's all black and white. What you see is what you get. Is this some kind of religious school or something?" Thomas asked, arching an eyebrow.

Castel smirked at that. "No, nothing like that. But if you really think the world is that simple, you're in for one hell of a surprise."

The remark unsettled Thomas. It left something twisting deep inside him—something uncertain and cold. Where exactly was Castel taking him? And what did he mean by a *hell of a surprise*?

They continued down a gravel path that led into the forest. The trees thickened, their canopies intertwining until they formed a dense ceiling, shading the path and cooling the air. The deeper they walked, the more the woods felt unfamiliar. No other students ventured this far; signs posted along the path warned of immediate expulsion beyond this point.

Security cameras blinked from hidden nooks in the branches, intensifying the sense of secrecy. Thomas's anxiety sharpened. Maybe that cult rumor had some merit after all. His stomach churned, his pulse quickened, and a tight discomfort settled in his gut.

Eventually, they reached a structure tucked within the trees, a small stone temple, modest in size, no larger than a garage. Four thick pillars stood at its corners, partially enveloped by the surrounding stone walls. A flat roof bore an iron emblem of two crossed axes and a round shield, reminiscent of something out of the Renaissance.

"What is this?" Thomas asked, eyeing the iron door warily.

"This," Castel said smoothly, approaching the entrance, "is

the way to the school."

A strange scent drifted from the door: salt and a sea breeze, like an ocean shore. But they were landlocked.

Castel opened the heavy door and gestured for Thomas to step inside. From where he stood, Thomas could see a torch-lit staircase spiraling downward like something from a catacomb.

Cult. I'm dead. This is my death, Thomas thought. He stepped forward cautiously, each footfall heavier than the last. By the time he reached the threshold, his legs felt like cement blocks. He froze. The image of a horror movie flashed in his mind, and suddenly, dying in a cult didn't seem as exciting as it had from the safety of a screen.

Before he could turn back, Castel gave him a firm push. Thomas stumbled forward, catching himself a few steps down.

Crossing the temple's threshold sent a shiver down his spine. A strange sensation washed over him as if some unseen weight had been lifted. His hair felt brittle, and the air tasted different. Castel followed, closing the door behind them with a solid metallic click. The sound echoed ominously.

The feeling reminded Thomas of the calming tea Castel had given him in the principal's office. Relaxed and oddly clear-headed, he accepted the sensation.

Castel had already begun his descent into the torch-lit tunnel. Thomas followed deeper into the catacomb-like stairwell. He wanted to ask questions but feared the answers would confirm his worst suspicions. In his mind, he was already dead.

By the time he reached the bottom, his thighs were burning, his breath ragged, his shirt clinging to his back. *Torture before death. Lovely,* he thought, keeping his expression blank.

They stepped into a large circular chamber. Thomas stood on one of five staircases, each emerging from different points around the room. Directly ahead stood a massive wooden door adorned with painted runes.

The chamber was ancient rough stone walls carved sporadically with runic symbols, layered and worn as though added over centuries.

Thomas stared at the runes framing the door. . He squinted, translating slowly: "Welcome to your new home."

"The thought of living in this dungeon..." Thomas muttered, "Yeah. I'm definitely screwed."

"Wow, Castel, can your student read Elder Futhark?" a new voice said.

Startled, Thomas turned. A sharp-looking man with spiky white hair stood to the left. Beside him, a girl around Thomas's age with tan skin, curly brown hair, and serious eyes studied him through her glasses. She wore shorts and a look of caution.

Their eyes met. Thomas looked away quickly.

"Sure can," Castel replied proudly. "We've been teaching it at Blackwood."

"Blackwood Academy?" the girl asked, surprised. "You came all the way here? That's, like, two hundred miles."

"Two hundred what? No, we just walked behind the school through the forest," Thomas replied.

She gave him a look like he'd grown a third eye. Castel exchanged a quiet glance with his white-haired companion.

"Woah! Is that Futhark?" a voice boomed from the right.

A lanky, sleep-deprived man with glasses appeared, trailed by a tall, athletic boy around Thomas's age.

"I can't read it, but that's sick," the boy said. "Oh man, how do we get to the school from here? Bet it's gonna be wild!"

Thomas sighed. The guy still thought this was a school tour. *We're about to be fed to some Viking god,* he thought grimly.

Tension filled the room; the mentors were watching, and the kids were uneasy.

"Alright, everyone, step up to the door," Castel said, clapping once. The sound echoed off the stone walls. Thomas flinched. He glanced at the other two teens: the jock looked far too excited while the girl shared his unease.

Still, Thomas stepped forward first. The other two followed.

"Last goodbyes," he said. "I'm Thomas."

"Mari," the girl responded flatly, not amused.

"Brody's the name," the jock grinned, slapping Thomas on the back hard enough to jolt him forward.

Silence fell again.

"Open," Castel commanded.

The door creaked slowly on its hinges, revealing a sunlit campus beyond a vast schoolyard bustling with students. A warm and salty ocean breeze swept over them.

Dumbfounded, they stepped through.

Ahead were sprawling dormitories and, far off, a towering main school building.

Thomas turned to Castel in disbelief. The doorway was gone. Behind them lay only an endless ocean and the stone platform they now stood on.

No way back.

And for the first time in what felt like years... Thomas smiled.

4

MAGIC ACADEMY

Still standing in awe, Thomas, Mari, and Brody couldn't help but be starstruck by the towering school before them. Slowly, Thomas took the first step only to be met by none other than Castel, striding toward them from the right.

They all instinctively turned back to glance at where the doorway had been. Castel's arrival from a different direction was strange yet oddly fitting in a world that was already rewriting their understanding of reality.

Castel no longer wore his formal suit. Instead, he had on a pair of jeans and a black button-up shirt, unfastened to reveal a fitted undershirt. Bracelets lined his wrists, and dog tags hung from his neck. His chestnut hair matched the purple of his eyes, and a warm smile spread across his face as he greeted them.

"Welcome to your new home. Right here is where legends once stood Triangle Academy. Named, of course, after our location."

Thomas blinked. "Wait, our location? What does that mean?"

He was cut off by Mari's voice, sharp with realization. "We're in the Bermuda Triangle?" she asked, her tone a blend of disbelief and wonder.

Brody's eyes lit up. "I always wondered where the school was! My parents told me I'd find out when I arrived."

Thomas made a mental note. Brody seemed familiar with this world, possibly born into it or initiated at a certain age. Mari, however, was more like him, lost and confused. Still, she had one clear advantage: intelligence. She radiated it. She might even be the smartest among them.

"Correct!" Castel beamed. "We are, in fact, in the Bermuda Triangle. This academy sits on a wellspring of powerful magic, where the human and magical realms brush against each other."

He began walking backward, hands gesturing animatedly as he led them forward.

"You're standing on the Portal Platform," he explained. "This is where all newcomers and outside guests arrive. Behind me, what we're walking into now is the schoolyard."

Thomas caught only pieces of the speech, his attention too fixed on the vibrant, surreal world unfolding around him. This place, pulled straight from fiction and fantasy, shouldn't have existed. And yet, here it was.

The yard was expansive, like a national park. Trees, benches, and barbecue grills dotted the open field. Buildings on both sides lined the perimeter in a massive U-shape, all pristine and modern-looking. The surrounding dorms were impressive, five stories tall, but the academy itself soared above them, easily ten stories high. From where Thomas stood, it looked like it could house an entire city.

They walked a clean stone pathway through the yard toward the main campus. Students filled the space, dressed in everyday clothes. Some played frisbee, others read under trees or strummed instruments. Strangely, Thomas didn't feel the usual weight dragging in his mind. The dull ache in his head was gone. He felt...light.

Is this what hope feels like? He wondered. His face ached from smiling. He wanted to laugh. It felt impossible that this was real.

They finally reached the main campus, where dormitories met the academy proper. Stepping inside, they were immediately hit by a swirl of mouth watering aromas. Thomas caught the scent of Korean BBQ, fried chicken, and pizza. His stomach growled so loudly that Castel even chuckled.

"Okay, okay, I get it," Castel grinned. "Go grab something quickly. We'll keep walking, but food on the go is fine."

Thomas blushed while Brody whooped. "Hell yeah, food!" he shouted, charging toward the buffet.

Mari lingered with Castel, but Thomas followed Brody, eyes scanning the spread. It was set up cafeteria-style, with trays and to-go boxes. And then he saw it.

Spiced Honey-Glazed Bread.

His favorite. Cheap and warm and familiar. Something he'd smuggled from Blackwood for himself and Samuel. Something he could always count on. He moved toward it like it was calling his name. The loaf glistened with honey, its dense body flecked with cinnamon, nutmeg, and just enough chili to give it a gentle kick.

He picked it up with both hands, letting the honey drip down his fingers. Tearing off a piece, he popped it into his mouth. Tears welled in his eyes. It was better than he remembered. Magic was great, but this? This was comfortable. Maybe even healing.

He returned to the others holding just the bread. Mari arched her brow. Castel laughed.

"An entire loaf?" Mari asked, puzzled.

Castel chuckled louder. "Still just bread, even here? I thought that was a Blackwood budget thing. Turns out you just really *love* that stuff!"

Brody appeared with a plate stacked so high the lid wouldn't close. "Wait, why do you *only* have bread?" he asked, bewildered.

No one answered. They just laughed.

The tour resumed, winding through the academy's interior. The lower floors resembled high school science labs and traditional classrooms, but by the fifth floor, things changed.

Floor 5 was tangled with thick, living vines. Floor 6 was frozen, icy, and brittle. Floor 7 cracked with dry heat and sweltering air. Thomas almost felt sick from the rapid climate shifts. Thankfully, Floor 8 was normal, with its tiered classrooms built like amphitheaters.

To their surprise, the academy wasn't empty for summer. Many students were around, especially older seniors like Castel, whose presence felt both inspiring and intimidating.

Floors 9 and 10 held enormous libraries, vast study halls, and even a battle arena. The space seemed impossibly vast compared to the outside view.

But Castel wasn't done.

He led them away from the campus, down a dirt path through rolling fields. Far in the distance, a vast forest loomed. But closer still was a sprawling farm. Castel pointed to it, smiling.

"Where are we going?" Mari asked quietly.

"To the farm," Castel replied, cheerful. "You'll see. Magical creatures aren't like the animals you know. We have some... very special pets."

Excitement sparked in Thomas. What kind of beasts lived here? Phoenixes? Dragons? How far did this magical world stretch?

At last, they reached the barn, and the sight took their breath away.

Beyond the fence stood creatures the size of horses, resembling deer. Glowing runes marked their naturally formed antlers, which burned faintly red at the tips and flickered with ember-like sparks. Their eyes were dark as coal. Their coats were grey, streaked with glowing red fissures.

One opened its mouth and breathed fire.

Thomas started, speechless. This wasn't fiction. This was his new reality.

Walking up to them was a cat, except it had butterfly wings. It flapped them gently, lifting its small body into the air while licking its paw. Slowly, it floated over to Brody, who grinned with delight, only for the cat to smack him across the cheek and hiss before flying off at a leisurely pace.

"What did I do?!" Brody exclaimed, rubbing his cheek.

"Nothing. That's just cats for you," Castel teased as they continued toward the barn.

Along the side of the fence, they passed massive, bug-eyed lizards fitted with saddles and small, dragon-like creatures the size of dogs darting and leaping through the grass. But when they reached the barn entrance, the atmosphere shifted.

Each stall inside was sealed behind reinforced glass, and warning signs plastered across every door read, "DO NOT ENTER. DEAD INSIDE."

The group froze. Mari finally broke the silence. "What is this?"

Castel was quiet for a moment, gathering his thoughts.

"Honestly... I want you to see both the good and the bad. This is a magical world. There are things here that can kill you. People who can kill you with a flick of their wrist. It's not all sunshine and rainbows," he said softly, stepping up to one of the enclosures.

The label read: Stalkers.

Inside, sleek, panther-like creatures paced strikingly eyeless. They shimmered and flickered, disappearing from one spot and reappearing in another, blinking in and out of existence.

"These are Stalkers. Similar to panthers from the human world, but time behaves differently with them. They have magical abilities like we do, and they can shift through time, freeze it, and play it." Castel's voice had taken on a colder, more somber edge.

Thomas's eyes widened. If these creatures could manipulate time... could they?

"So... what other kinds of magic are there?" he asked. "If time magic exists, what about space?"

"Silence," Castel snapped his fingers.

Thomas flinched at the harsh tone.

"There are kinds of magic that are forbidden because of their power and others that are outright illegal. Ordinary mages can't access forbidden magic. It's passed down through bloodlines," Castel said, his tone softening. "And there are strict policies around even talking about that type of magic unless you're a trained professional. I didn't mean to snap. It's just... a sensitive subject for a lot of people."

Thomas gave him a slight, understanding nod. Brody rested a reassuring hand on his shoulder. Mari and Brody both looked visibly shaken by the shift in mood.

The tour continued, leading them away from the barn and back toward the academy. Thomas chewed on a piece of bread, trying to regain some confidence. The walk was quiet, weighed down by the tension between them.

Mari's eyes drifted toward the trees. "What about the forest?" she asked timidly, unsure whether Castel would lash out again.

"That's still school property," Castel said gently. "Sometimes animals wander in so that it can be dangerous. It's not off-limits but like any forest... you never know what's in it."

The silence resumed, broken only by the laughter of other students playing around the campus.

As they approached the portal platform in the main yard, the dorms came into view. The left side was for the girls, and the right was for the boys. It was time to split up.

Mari smiled at them. "Hey guys, it was nice meeting you!" she called out, waving.

Thomas and Brody returned the gesture with warm smiles as Castel led the boys inside the massive foyer of the male dormitory.

The interior featured impressive cozy seating scattered across the room, with couches, bean bags, and armchairs. Tables lined the walls for studying. There was a small kitchen with coffee makers, Keurigs, microwaves, air fryers, and a communal fridge, though it was completely empty, suggesting students didn't share often.

As they continued walking, Thomas saw cloudy windows revealing a full gym, a sauna, and even a swimming pool. A smaller gymnasium sat nearby with just half a basketball court, suitable for tennis or other casual games.

But what truly lit up Thomas's face was the massive arcade packed with retro and modern games. There was even a quiet library stocked with leisure books and a soundproof reading room.

"This place is insane," Thomas whispered.

"Dude, they got a weight room!" Brody said, grabbing Thomas by the shoulders.

"Nah, Nah, did you see that arcade? That was amazing!" Thomas pushed him back, grinning wide.

Castel just smiled at their excitement. They stepped into the elevator and rode it up, the hallway buzzing with activity. Boys wandered out of showers with towels around their waists, some in boxers, doors wide open. It wasn't unfamiliar for Thomas. He'd grown up in an orphanage, but the age gap made him feel out of place.

Finally, Castel stopped in front of a door.

"This is your room, Brody. Your roommate's name is Silas. He's a good kid, quiet," he said, smiling.

Thomas waved as Brody disappeared into the room. He already missed his energy, and it had been comforting.

"Castel, what's my roommate like?" Thomas asked.

"Elias. Bit of a nerd, but fun. Loves magic and studying. Honestly, I think he's perfect for you, given your limited experience with this world." Castel's tone wasn't insulting, but it stung a little.

"Are we the only new kids?" Thomas asked.

Castel chuckled, shaking his head. "Not at all. But you two were the last ones we recruited. My classmates and I weren't even sure we'd find anyone this year. But James insisted he sensed a presence, and then we found you."

He stopped and placed a hand on Thomas's shoulder. "You've got a lot to learn. But you're special."

Thomas's chest warmed. He smiled, cheeks reddening.

They reached the door, Room 525. A chill crept over him, nerves bubbling as he reached for the handle.

"Thank you, Castel... for everything this summer."

Then, with a deep breath, Thomas opened the door.

5

MARI

One Week Prior

To assume the world treats everyone the same or that we all walk in identical shoes is naïve. Thomas, who had nothing, was being offered the opportunity of a lifetime. For Mari, however, life had always been more forgiving. She had a family, a boyfriend, and a comfortable life. Her world wasn't scarred by hardship the way Thomas's was. She enjoyed her quiet routines, even if it meant burying her nose in books to understand the world.

Mari attended a public school.

"Go Tigers!" a cheerleader shouted, twirling in the center of the basketball court.

The crowd barely responded to a few grunts and scattered claps. Most students looked bored or distracted, attending orientation more out of obligation than excitement. Cheerleaders and sports teams paraded across the gymnasium, performing their annual attempts to pump up school spirit, acting like local celebrities rather than students.

Mari sat in the back corner of the bleachers, her focus on the book in her lap. Beside her, a boy tapped away on a handheld gaming console, yawning.

"What are you reading?" he asked, raising an eyebrow. His name was Jordan, and he had been her boyfriend since summer. Their story was the classic "best friends to lovers" trope, only without the spark. Three months in, and it felt more like a lukewarm friendship than a passionate romance. They had kissed, sure, but that was about the only difference.

Mari glanced over her glasses at him. "*Mages, Myths, or Reality,*" she said, turning the book so he could see the cover.

It was plain white, with a faint blue aura surrounding a Viking rune symbol.

"Ha. Mages, huh? That's tight. If magic were real, I'd probably be the strongest of them all," Jordan said, puffing up his ego like always. He often acted like he'd be the hero in any dangerous situation even though he had never so much as thrown a punch.

Mari rolled her eyes and returned to her reading.

The book spoke of Algernon's Vikings whose histories were passed down orally until eventually recorded in cryptic texts. The author, Allen Joel, was a mystery himself; whenever Mari searched for him online, there were no results. Stranger still, she had found the book inside her locker. There was no logical way it could have fit through the slots. Still, with everything strange happening lately, Mari had stopped questioning what was possible.

She didn't feel grounded in her school life anymore. Puberty had brought more than mood swings or awkward changes; it brought something supernatural. Her fingertips hummed with yellow energy, drawing knowledge straight from the book's pages and embedding it in her mind.

Her eyes flicked toward the faculty seats across the gym, locking on Lee, an advisor who had been watching her closely for weeks. She could feel it in his aura. He was like her.

She watched a ribbon of golden energy drift from his body, snake across the gym floor, and then crawl up the wall toward her. As her fingers brushed the wood beside her, she *felt* his message absorb into her thoughts.

Meet me after orientation.

She didn't react outwardly. Their eyes met across the gym. He nodded. She nodded back.

The rest of the orientation blurred by. Pep talks, team introductions, and school expectations - none of them mattered to Mari. Lee told her not to focus on this school but never said why. Maybe now he finally would.

When the final bell rang, the gym exploded into chatter and stomping feet. Jordan turned to her.

"Let's go, sweetie."

Something about the way he said it made her stomach turn. She didn't hate him. But he never treated her like a partner. He acted like they were still just buddies. She hesitated.

"I'll... meet up with you later," she said softly.

"Cool," he mumbled, already focused on his game as he wandered off.

She lingered behind, slowly packing her book away, killing time until she was alone. Finally, she made her way to the double doors and stepped into the hallway, where Lee was waiting by the trophy case.

"Well, howdy, howdy, Mari. Seems like you're starting to tap into your mage side," he said, flashing a grin. His white hair was spiked and brilliant against his pale skin, and his tailored suit made him look both charming and slightly dangerous.

"What do you want, Lee?" Mari asked, crossing her arms.

"It's time. We leave tonight."

Mari's eyes widened. "The hell do you mean *tonight?*" she said, pushing him lightly.

"Ow damn. I mean your new school. The board already spoke with your parents. They're... persuasive," Lee replied, handing her a pamphlet from his jacket.

She took it cautiously and flipped through the photos. It was breathtaking. Too perfect to be real.

"Does it *have* to be tonight?" she asked anxiously.

"Well... the last day for admission is a week from now."

"Can I push it off till then?"

Lee hesitated. "I guess. Can I ask why?"

Mari took a breath. "I have a life here. I need to say goodbye."

Lee softened, resting a hand on her shoulder. "During the summers and holidays, you can come home. And with your ability to use dimensional doors... Well, you can come and go anytime."

Mari blushed and pushed his hand off.

"Fine. Just... give me the week."

She looked away, voice dropping. "And... will I be the only one like me? Half-mage?"

Lee sighed. "Yes. You're rare. Mages have strict laws about breeding while retaining magic. If your father had renounced his powers first... things might've been different. But it doesn't matter anymore."

His voice dimmed, and with it, so did Mari's heart.

Her nails pressed into her palms.

Her father, his execution, her powers erupting for the first time, and the mage alert system, how their auras reacted to one another, like wolves scenting blood.

She forced a smile. "Right. I'll be ready in a week."

Lee nodded, smiling. "Sounds like a plan"

"What are you doing here with him, Mari?"

Jordan's voice cut through the hallway. He stood there, gripping his game system. Lee's hand snapped back as he quickly backed away.

"I'mma leave you to it. See you next week," he muttered and vanished down the hall.

"Are you cheating on me? Is this why you've been distant?"

Mari massaged her temples as Jordan continued his rant.

"Jordan." Her voice was calm, but when she pointed at him, the world fell silent.

No sound left his lips, though his mouth moved.

She sighed. The golden aura surrounding them shimmered, muting the chaos. Finally, she met his gaze and lifted the spell.

"I would have done anything for you!" he finished.

But Mari had already made her decision.

One Week Later

She'd said her goodbyes. Hugged friends. Let go of her town. Leaving her mom was the hardest. Her mother had stood by her since the execution, and if she hadn't supported this decision, Mari wouldn't have left.

Now, with a backpack slung over her shoulder and two suitcases in hand, she stepped into the living room where Lee waited.

Her mother smiled softly and pulled her into a long embrace. "I'll miss you," she said, voice trembling.

"I'll visit whenever I can," Mari replied. She was nearly her mother's height, and soon, she might surpass her.

"I'll take great care of her, I promise," Lee added.

"I trust you. Though I have no idea what I'm going to do with all this free time," her mom said, attempting humor.

"Maybe try dating?" Mari teased.

Her mother laughed. "Oh, sweetie. Your father was the only one for me."

Mari smiled through the tears. "I love you."

"I love you too, sweet pea."

She lingered one last moment, touching the photo of her father above the fireplace. His golden ring with an engraved hourglass rested beside it. He'd worn it every day. Her fingers brushed the frame before she turned to go.

Lee led her down a few blocks to the old graveyard. They descended into an ordinary tomb on the outside, but inside, the stone corridor stretched deep underground, torch-lit and ancient. This was the same day, perhaps even the exact moment when Thomas was discovering his path. And Mari wondered: Had her father known? Was this why they lived so close?

She stepped into the underground chamber and met Thomas's eyes.

Present Day

Mari walked the dormitory hallway, nerves buzzing. She reached her door, knocked three times, and stepped inside.

A bright, bubbly girl with black hair and a broad smile greeted her.

"Oh. My. God! You must be my roommate!" she squealed.

Mari blinked, unintentionally making a face.

"I'm Mari. Nice to meet you," she said, offering a handshake. Her gaze drifted across the room. One side was neatly organized and neutral. The other? Drenched in pink, covered in posters, stuffies, and plushies.

"I'm Eva!" the girl beamed. "I tried to keep my stuff to my side. But if you like the vibe, I have *plenty* more to share!"

Mari smiled gently, appreciating that Eva wasn't pushing anything on her. "I appreciate it, Eva. I'm okay, though, thank you."

As she unpacked, Mari couldn't help but feel a spark of hope. If she could get along with Eva, who was her complete opposite, maybe she could learn to open up here.

6

FOOTBALL, MAGIC, BRODY

The stadium lights blazed above him, hot and blinding, sweat pooling beneath Brody's brow. His eyes cut through the sea of chanting fans:

"Lions! Lions! Lions!"

The bleachers shook with stomping feet. Brody stood poised, hands ready to receive the ball. His heart thudded against his chest, but unlike most, this wasn't anxiety. For Brody, this was home. The only thing he did better than football... was breathing.

The scent of fresh-cut grass, the chill of the night breeze, and the weight of the dirt on his jersey grounded him. This moment was peace.

All I do is win, he thought, a grin curling in his mind. *This is nothing.*

His feet shifted, breath steady, eyes scanning the defense.

"HIKE!"

His voice cracked through the roar. The score was tied. Seconds on the clock. Exactly how he wanted it.

Brody thrived in the pressure. He loved the drama, the glory, the story everyone would tell. An underdog playing to win nationals? A plaque on the school wall? That was Brody's design.

The ball snapped into his hands. He stepped back, scanning the field. He already knew who he'd target: Theo, a quiet, fragile kid barely on the team. A filler. No one expected anything from him.

But Brody? Brody would make him a legend.

Theo sprinted for the end zone, untouched. Brody's arm whipped back and released the ball, which soared like a bird, glowing faintly with a soft yellow shimmer. Magic, subtle but deliberate. It altered the ball's arc just slightly.

From the corner of his eye, Brody caught sight of his coach, furious on the sideline. His teammates clutched their heads in disbelief. The buzzer screamed.

And then the ball slammed perfectly into Theo's arms.

Silence followed, brief and deafening. Brody heard nothing but the hum in his ears; his aura strained to guide the ball.

Then the explosion came.

The crowd roared. Teammates rushed the field. His coach burst into laughter, tossing his clipboard. Brody stood there, helmet in hand, sweat rolling down his temples. He'd done it. National champions.

But in the crowd, his eyes found his father.

The disapproving stare hit him harder than any tackle.

He could guess why. The magic. Not because it broke the rules but because the glory wasn't all his. Brody had shared the moment with someone weak, and that disgusted his father more than the magic itself.

The celebration lost its taste. Brody slipped away, the buzz in his ears replaced by the cold silence of the car. His father sat across from him, arms crossed.

"You could have won that yourself," he said flatly.

Brody looked down. He knew it. Yellow magic for speed and strength spells, he could have done alone. But Theo needed it more. That touchdown would change the boy's life.

He didn't respond. Neither did his father.

They arrived home, the car pulling into the circular driveway of their mansion. Brody trailed behind as his father stepped inside. The freshly mopped tiles gleamed under the light. He turned to take the stairs, pausing outside his parents' room.

His mother stood at the mirror, fixing her makeup, wine in hand.

"I saw the game," she said without turning. "I watched through your father's eyes. Go shower. You look awful."

Her voice was cold, detached.

Brody turned away, retreating to his room to prepare for dinner. Every meal in that house tasted perfect. But nothing about it ever felt warm.

He sat at one end of the long table, dressed in a clean button-up tucked into his jeans. The dinner had been delayed for his game, but it didn't matter. His father's silence said it all.

Then came the words.

"Brody," his father announced. "The Academy has officially recruited you."

The pride in his voice struck Brody harder than anything else. Not the offer he'd expected. His father's influence guaranteed it. But to hear pride? Real pride?

"You won't have football distracting you anymore," his father continued. "This is the big leagues now."

Brody's mother chimed in: "Don't disappoint us. Our family

name rides on you.”

He nodded. “Yes, sir. Yes, ma’am.”

But he wondered if they had ever shown him love when he was small. Did they ever cradle him the way other parents did? He wished he could remember.

“I won’t,” he whispered. “I’ll make you proud.”

Their silence gave him no answer.

He shoveled food into his mouth, using the taste to drown the ache in his chest. If only the perfection around him extended to the people who raised him.

Arrival at the Academy

Later that night, Brody stepped out the mansion’s back door into a small temple tucked away on the estate. He descended the familiar stairs. A portal shimmered ahead, one of many his family had access to.

He barely spoke to the student guiding him. His thoughts were elsewhere until he saw them: two others waiting in the tomb chamber.

Mari and Thomas.

Mari’s aura flickered with potential, strong but not unique. Thomas, though? Something was off. No aura. No scent of magic. Clean. Too clean.

Why was someone like that here?

Eventually, he was left at the door to his new room, exhausted from the journey. He turned the knob, pushed it open, and froze.

A shaggy redhead stared back at him. Thin, freckled, nervous.

"Roommates!" Brody grinned, tossing his luggage onto his bed. "Oh man, we're gonna be best buds."

The boy jumped at the sound. "Silas," he said, offering a shy hand.

Brody slammed his hand into it, shaking so hard that Silas's teeth rattled.

The room was lined with magical biology artifacts, including wingless dragon skulls and behemoth geckos in jars. Brody glanced around. He'd expected to be alone, but this was fine.

"Are you into biology?" he asked.

Silas blushed. "N-no. I'm specializing in summoning magic. I want to work at a sanctuary for magical creatures, not experiment on them."

His voice was timid, but there was a spark in his eyes.

Brody grinned, slapping him on the arm. Silas winced.

"Hell yeah, brother. I don't have a specialty yet. Might do a transmutation."

That raised Silas's eyebrows. Transmutation was elite magic that was rare and dangerous. Only the most powerful could handle three creature attributes. Most managed just one. A few, two. Summoning, Silas's path, was more common. Still, stories told of ancient mages who summoned hundreds of beasts in wartime. Legends. Or so people said.

As Brody unpacked, they talked more. Magical creatures. Their families. Silas came from an old Mage line. So did Brody.

For the first time in a long while, Brody felt like he wasn't alone.

7

ELIAS THE KNOWLEDGEABLE

Thomas pushed open the door to his room. His eyes felt heavy, and he was slightly dazed. He wasn't sure what to expect, but to his surprise, the room was empty. Blinking a few times in disbelief, he glanced around, briefly wondering if he had the wrong room. Scratching the back of his head, he hesitantly stepped through the doorway.

The moment he did, a wave of something wet and slimy wrapped around him. It felt like stepping through a bubble sticky and unpleasant on his skin. Once he was fully inside, the ooze slid off him and snapped back like elastic, wobbling slightly. Then he saw him, Elias, sitting at a desk, reading.

Books were scattered across Elias's side of the room, titles like *The History of Mages*, *The Magical Society*, and even *World History*, which seemed out of place among the rest.

Thomas glanced back at the doorway. Outside, people passed by without sparing a glance. His heart raced. This was real. This strange, magical world was now his reality.

"It's a ward," Elias said suddenly without looking up. "It

keeps people from seeing us or entering unless they meet my criteria." His voice was calm and slightly nasally. He had short, thick black hair combed up in the front, and he wore black-rimmed glasses with a faint purple tint in the right light.

"I don't know what any of that means..." Thomas stammered, anxiety fluttering in his stomach. He felt the urgent need to use the restroom.

"You don't." Elias paused, then set his book down and looked at Thomas properly. "You must not be from the world of mages."

Thomas gave a sheepish nod.

"A ward is a form of protection. Historically, it referred to a fortress enclosed by walls. In our case, it's magic placed on the doorframe. It stops unwanted visitors and alerts me if someone tries to enter who doesn't belong."

Thomas blinked, still processing. "Will it always feel like that when I enter?"

"No," Elias replied simply, turning back to his book.

Thomas dropped his backpack to the floor and climbed onto his bed. It was soft and squishy, like sinking into a marshmallow. As he lay back, the pillow molded around his head.

"This must be what magic is all about," he sighed.

Elias glanced over, confused. "These are just normal." He stopped and smirked, refocusing on his book. It was clear Elias knew more about Thomas than he let on and was choosing to tread lightly.

Thomas's eyes grew heavy. He had never lain on a bed this soft. He took a deep breath, exhaling slowly.

"The name's Thomas," he said, opening his eyes.

But he wasn't in the dorm anymore.

Panic set in. He tried to sit up, but something held him down. He looked around frantically. He was strapped to a cold, metal table in a grey-bricked room. Blood stained the tiles. A burning sensation spread through his body. He arched his back in agony as glowing purple hands emerged from the shadows, pressing down on him. It felt like his bones were turning to ash.

He screamed raw, guttural, and loud as tears streamed down his face.

"THOMAS!"

His eyes flew open. He bolted upright and crashed to the floor.

Elias, in pajamas, stood near the desk. Early morning sunlight streamed through the window. Thomas lay on his stomach, scrambling to his feet and backing into the corner, trembling and tear-streaked.

"Thomas, hey, are you okay?" Elias asked gently, one hand raised like calming a wild animal. "You were screaming like you were dying."

Thomas looked at the bed. It was soaked in sweat.

Breathing heavily, he slid to the floor and rested his head against the wall. "I'm sorry," he muttered.

Elias knelt beside him. "It's fine. They gave me some info when you were assigned to me. But... they never mentioned night terrors."

"I've never had night terrors before," Thomas admitted. He rubbed his face, trying to compose himself. "I'm gonna take a shower."

Elias nodded, guiding Thomas to the floor's bathroom. The hallway was quiet, and most students were still asleep after a long night of excitement. But not Thomas.

Staring at his reflection in the mirror, Thomas tried to breathe. His eyes were sunken, his skin pale, hair greasy. He clenched his teeth, exposing discolored enamel. He hadn't brushed them in days. Hygiene had become an afterthought.

He brushed his teeth, spat, and splashed cold water on his face to jolt his brain awake.

The hot shower hit his skin like heaven. He hadn't felt water this warm in years. At the orphanage, he always gave the younger kids first dibs especially in winter.

Tears welled up as the heat soaked into him. People forgot how much the little things could mean.

After drying off, he threw on a red-and-black flannel and brushed his shaggy auburn bangs out of his eyes. Back in the hallway, other students were waking up. Some had objects floating around them, books, trays, and even a toothbrush brushing one kid's teeth for him.

Returning to the room, he found Elias fully dressed in jeans and a loose hoodie that looked more like a T-shirt.

"Hey," Elias said, "I know you're new to the mage world. Let's grab some breakfast. You can ask me anything."

Thomas exhaled in relief. For once, someone was willing to help.

Outside, the summer morning breeze brushed his skin. As they walked to the cafeteria, Thomas wondered about Brody and Mari. Were their roommates as kind as Elias?

The cafeteria was nearly empty. Thomas piled bacon, eggs, sausage, and pancakes onto his tray. At the table, Elias sipped black coffee and read while Thomas devoured his food in silence.

After chugging a glass of orange juice, Thomas wiped his mouth on his sleeve. "So... when does school start?"

"Tomorrow," Elias said. "Today's for settling in. There'll be a pre-show event tonight, games, fun, a chance to meet people."

Thomas wrinkled his nose at the coffee. "How do you drink that black stuff so casually? It just feels wrong."

Elias chuckled.

"What do I need to know about this world?" Thomas asked.

Elias paused, lowering his book. "Alright. Let's dive in."

The next hour flew by. Elias explained that the magical world was descended from the Algernons, an ancient Viking tribe gifted with powers by the gods. Magic was drawn from a person's aura, its color reflecting its type: red for fire, blue for water, yellow for augmentation, brown for earth, and green for nature. Shades and tints varied with specialization.

By the end, Thomas's brain felt like pudding.

"Can we please take a break?" he groaned, rubbing his temples. "I appreciate it, man, but you're frying my brain."

Suddenly, he coughed and slammed into the table as a sting shot up his back.

Brody stood behind him, grinning. "Yo yo, what's up!"

"Hey, Brody," Thomas wheezed.

"This is Brody," Thomas said, gesturing. "Brody, my room-mate Elias."

Brody leaned over and smacked Elias's arm. "Howdy howdy, nice to meet ya!"

Behind him stood another boy with unkempt, dark red hair. "Name's Silas," he muttered, cutting Brody's intro short.

"Nice to meet you, Silas," Thomas said. "We came here together."

Brody slapped Thomas's chest, making him gasp. "Whoa, look at that beauty!"

The others winced in sympathy. A girl with black hair in a ponytail skipped by with a plate of biscuits and gravy. She was bubbly, over-the-top and gorgeous by Brody's standards.

Before Brody could start drooling, Mari's hand smacked his head. "Stop staring, fool. Eva! Over here!"

Eva beamed and skipped over, placing her plate next to Silas and sitting beside him. "Oh my God, are you guys friends with Mari?"

"Absolutely!" Brody beamed.

Mari took the seat next to Thomas. Now he was surrounded by Mari on one side, Eva beside her, Silas, Elias, and Brody on the other.

For the first time, Thomas was part of something people chose to sit with *him*.

"Mari is so much fun! She's the coolest!" Eva gushed.

Everyone at the table was different. Silas, like Thomas, wore a flannel though tighter jeans. Brody was in basketball shorts and a T-shirt. Elias looked academic. Mari had on jeans and a band tee, while Eva wore a skirt, leggings, and a colorful blouse.

Was the school pairing opposites on purpose?

Thomas looked at Elias's glasses, black coffee, and books. He, meanwhile, was clueless.

Before he could say more, a hand landed on his shoulder.

Castel stood above him, smiling.

"Looks like someone finally made some friends," Castel teased.

"I had plenty," Thomas shot back, smirking.

Mari froze, eyes locked on Castel. His earrings, black skinny jeans, and button-up shirt tucked in all caught her attention. She barely noticed Brody's banter or Eva's glee.

"Mari," Castel said, and she snapped to attention.

"Brody. Thomas. And...?"

"Elias."

"E-Eva!" she chirped.

A pause. "Silas," he added.

"Well, well. A fresh batch of newbies," Castel grinned. "Plans for your last day of freedom?"

Everyone exchanged glances. No one had made any.

"Me and Thomas are exploring. I'm giving him the Mage 101 tour," Elias offered.

Mari perked up. "Can I come? I'd love to know more!"

"Hell, why not all of us?" Castel said. "Let's get a head start on mage life."

Brody cheered. "Hell yeah, brother!"

"Sure," Silas agreed.

"Okay-y, but only because Mari's coming!" Eva chimed.

"Yeah, fine. Let's go," Elias said.

Within ten minutes, they were walking the campus together. For the first time in a long time, Thomas felt warmth in his chest.

He wasn't sure what he'd learned, but he was having a great time. He had *friends*.

As they wandered, laughter and jokes filled the air. Higher-level students practiced magic, one with a red aura blasting fire from his fingertips, another walking on air with a blue aura around his legs. That one got knocked down by a bird, sending his aura scattering.

"This is Castel, your air traffic controller," Castel mocked with a fake radio. "Please be aware of surroundings when flying."

Thomas's cheeks ached from smiling.

8

FESTIVAL TIME

As the day gradually faded into twilight, a soft orange hue blanketed the sky, and students began to gather in the courtyard. Castel led the way, ushering them into the open space with a grin.

"It's almost festival time," he announced.

The Festival was one of the academy's most anticipated events of the semester. It was an explosion of magic, food, vendors, and friendly competitions that brought the entire school together in celebration.

The group buzzed with excitement. Most of them had heard tales about the spectacle, but Mari and Thomas had only secondhand stories.

"I heard they once let a Pyro Mage create a dragon out of pure red aura!" Brody exclaimed, practically bouncing in place.

Thomas tried to follow along.

Pyromages... proficient in red magic. Red magic is the base form of fire magic other shades and hues give it different effects.

His mind worked to process the information. It was overwhelming, but after a full day of exploration, he was beginning to grasp the world he'd stepped into.

From the sidelines, Thomas watched teachers congregate at the center of the courtyard. Suddenly, a booming voice echoed across the island.

"Welcome, students! We are so happy to see so many bright, and beautiful faces this year and to welcome back so many of our returning stars! Who's ready for the fun?"

The crowd erupted in cheers. Even Castel whooped, caught in the contagious energy.

Brody let out a howl and shook Silas by the shoulders. "Let's gooo!"

Then, a surge of magic pulsed from the courtyard's center. A dazzling wave of energy washed over them, followed by an explosion of magical transformation.

Vendors, glowing lanterns, floating stages, and spectator stands bloomed into existence, forming a sprawling festival ground. The students didn't hesitate; they charged in, laughing and shouting with excitement.

Thomas stood frozen in awe.

Was this really his life now?

He wished Samuel could see it. He would've cried from joy.

"Let's go, guys!" Castel called, waving the group forward.

They stuck close as they weaved through crowds and dazzling sights. Animals, exotic foods, and magical games were a whirlwind of color and life.

Eva pointed excitedly at a nearby stall. "Over there! It's the Crystal Corns!"

"I heard they don't always show up at the festival. We have to try them," Brody added, grabbing Thomas's arm and pulling him toward the vendor.

The popcorn stand hissed and popped. Blue kernels burst into glowing orbs while a vendor crushed gemstones and sprinkled the dust on top. The light dimmed slightly, transforming the treat into something that resembled candied jewels.

Eva bought two bags, one for the girls and one for the boys. Brody opened his mouth to protest but thought better of it. He hadn't paid, after all.

The bag made its rounds until it reached Thomas. He scooped a handful and passed it to Castel. The kernels were hard in his hand, more like candy than popcorn.

He tossed a few into his mouth. Sweet, slightly savory, they melted into flavor as goosebumps prickled his arms.

Laughter and playful shoving broke out as the boys scrambled for more. Even Thomas found himself elbowing his way back for seconds.

Meanwhile, Eva and Mari were contentedly sharing their bag off to the side.

As the boys finished off their share, something else caught their attention.

"A pet stand!" someone shouted.

Silas shoved Brody aside and sped off. "Dude, I could've moved!" Brody huffed, brushing himself off as the group laughed and followed.

The stall was filled with fantastical creatures: echoing lynxes cats that repeated human phrases; butterfly felines with iridescent wings; rune-covered toads; and stonemadillos, armadillo-like creatures that turned to stone when startled.

"Can I buy a mystery orb?" Silas asked, handing over a crumpled twenty.

The orb would summon a random, miniature magical companion with no care or feeding required.

With a grin, Silas tossed it to the ground. It shattered like glass into dust. In its place stood a six-inch echo lynx, purring with bright curiosity.

"Bro, that thing's *sick*!" Brody said, amazed.

As if on cue, the lynx repeated, "Bro, that thing's *sick*!"

Laughter erupted. The other lynxes at the stall echoed the phrase in the chorus.

Brody's face turned pink. "Never mind. That's stupid."

Silas tried to stifle a laugh, the lynx now curled on his shoulder.

They continued to explore, moving from booth to booth. Thomas marveled at everything from blue noodles that changed flavor based on the eater's mood to charred skewers perfectly cooked with aura-infused fire.

A crowd was forming near a small stage. A boy around their age stood in the center, playing a violin.

"That's Noah Cross," someone said. "A music mage."

His aura rippled from the strings of his instrument, seeping into the crowd like an invisible mist. A sense of joy and anticipation settled over them.

As he played, students began dancing. A red-haired girl stepped into the center of Aziza Fey. Her body glowed with pink and yellow aura, her movements fluid and dazzling.

She spun and danced with impossible grace, eventually twisting onto her head and sliding into a dramatic finish as the music ended.

Cheers erupted.

"Did you see the hybrid magic she used?" Elias said, impressed.

"Is hybrid magic rare?" Mari asked.

"Not really," Eva replied. "But it's hard to control at our age.

Most of us can only use one type of magic."

"How did you know what color she used?" Thomas asked.

The group glanced at one another.

"You couldn't see her aura?" Elias asked.

Thomas shook his head.

"Late bloomer. Understandable," Brody said with a playful smack on Thomas's arm.

They moved on, but Elias lingered with a thoughtful look.

At the next booth, the group burst into a playful scuffle, racing to the front of the artifact vendor's tent.

Mari and Elias squeezed through the narrow entrance first.

Inside was a treasure trove of enchanted rings, scrolls, cloaks, shoes, and capes, each humming with magical energy.

"Well, howdy ho, partners!" called a tall, gangly man in a dusty shirt and jeans. He wore goggles over his eyes and sported a thick southern drawl.

"Name's Solomon Bright but y'all can call me Sol!"

"He's definitely from Texas," Mari whispered to Eva, who giggled.

Sol grinned wide. "Who's ready to spin the Wheel of Freedom? Win a prize, get a free magical item!"

Castel stepped into the tent, pausing at the sight.

"Sol. Don't scam them."

Sol flushed. "Now Castel, you wound me. This doesn't have anything to do with *last year*, does it?"

"Last year?" Mari asked, eager to hear about Castel's school life. Eva and Brody exchanged glances before looking back at her.

"Well," Castel began, folding his arms, "good old Sol here was supposed to make me a new pair of shoes. Not magical, just normal ones, since mine got wrecked during class. He gave them to me at the end of first year, and turns out, they were enchanted. I ran in them once over the summer, and they flew right off. Just took off into the sky!"

"Is *that* why you were in socks that one day during summer school?" Thomas smirked.

Castel rolled his eyes and nodded. "Exactly."

"Look," Sol interrupted, dragging a spinning wheel over to the register, "I won't *sell* them anything. But I *will* let them try their luck free artifact, handcrafted by yours truly!"

The group looked at each other. Brody, naturally, didn't hesitate. He grabbed the wheel and spun it with such force that the entire stand wobbled. The wheel spun furiously before finally slowing and landing on the golden arrow labeled FREE!

Sol clapped. "First win of the night! What do you want, big guy?"

As Brody inspected the table of magical trinkets, Elias and Silas politely declined a spin. Mari and Eva shook their heads as well, and then all eyes turned to Thomas. He hesitated. He was broke, but after a deep breath, he stepped forward and spun the wheel.

Click... click... click...

FREE!

"Nice!" someone in the group said, and a few claps followed.

"I feel like you two are going to get hurt," Mari muttered disapprovingly.

"Or maybe rich!" Eva grinned.

"Doubt it," Elias said, adjusting his glasses and pointing to an item on the table. "But that one's interesting."

Thomas followed his gaze to a cloak with a tag that read: *Modulates movement speed based on wearer's condition.*

"You think I should get it?" he asked.

Elias nodded, and Thomas picked it up.

"Good choice!" Sol beamed.

Brody snagged a fire-resistant cape.

"Oho! Another fine pick. You've got keen eyes, I'll give you that!" Sol clapped.

With that, the group headed out. Brody strutted with his black cape flaring behind him, looking like a high school basketball player accidentally dropped into medieval times. Thomas toyed with his cloak, flapping it around before slipping his arms through and adjusting the collar.

"Well?" Elias asked.

Thomas didn't answer. His head turned at a glacial pace. His mouth opened and the words came out slowly, distorted, like a bad video buffer.

"Definitely changed his speed," Castel groaned, slapping a hand to his forehead.

"Where to next?" Castel asked, eyeing the group. In the background, Thomas slowly peeled off the cloak, panting.

"There aren't a lot of older kids here," Silas noted.

"That's because most of them hang out at the competitive events," Castel explained. "The festival's fun, sure, but the older students are into serious stuff Tug-o-war, dodgeball, speed spellcasting, jousting..."

Brody's eyes lit up. "Did you say competition?" He slammed his fists together, grabbing Silas by the wrist. "Let's do it!"

Thomas finally caught his breath. "Really? No one helped me?"

"We figured you had it," Elias shrugged.

"Come on," Mari sighed. "Before Brody gets Silas killed."

They reached the competitive zone, a massive field divided into painted arenas for different games. A short line snaked past the signup booth. Older students were everywhere.

"Do the games stay the same every year?" Thomas asked.

Castel shook his head. "We always keep jousting, but the rest change. Sometimes we have basketball or baseball. They like to mix it up."

Before he could go on, Brody jogged back, clapping his hands.

"Alright! Thomas, Silas, Elias, and I are in for Tug-o-war and dodgeball!"

"WHAT?" the boys chorused.

The dodgeball match was first.

Thomas glanced at the stands. Castel waved. Mari stood beside him, blushing. Eva cheered and whistled.

On the field, Thomas joined Elias and Silas near the back. Brody stood front and center, practically vibrating with excitement.

"Cheer up, guys it'll be fun!" Brody grinned. Maybe for him, Thomas thought. The rest of them weren't exactly athletes.

The teacher, a muscular man in jeans and a tucked-in button-up, clapped his hands. "Same rules as normal dodgeball. Go!"

Their opponents were fellow first-years, thankfully. No overpowered upperclassmen.

Brody darted forward, grabbed two levitating orbs, and sprinted back, hurling one across the field. It exploded in a burst of wind as it hit a kid's face. The crowd roared.

Brody tossed a sphere to Thomas. "One down, three to go!"

Thomas managed a weak smile. "Alright, beefcake, let's try this."

He looked across the field. The first kid hit was now suspended in a glowing bubble.

"Watch out!" Elias shouted, shoving Thomas aside just in time to take a hit himself.

The sphere exploded, engulfing Elias in flames. Thomas froze.

"I'm fine! Illusion magic," Elias called, now resembling a walking fireball.

'This game is terrifying,' Thomas thought.

A sphere sailed toward Silas. He caught it clean. The crowd cheered.

"Hell yeah, brother!" Brody shouted.

Silas passed the orb to Brody. Two opponents left.

"Right side!" Brody called.

Thomas nodded, ran forward, and threw. His sphere missed, but Brody's didn't, slamming into the chest of the same kid. It exploded in a wave of water, drenching the opponent and washing him off the field.

"How do those things work?" Mari asked Castel.

"They're spell orbs, sugar glass infused with magic. When they break, the spell activates. Mostly illusions or pushback effects," he explained.

"WE HAVE A WINNER!" the teacher roared.

Thomas leaped into Brody's arms while fist pumping. Silas and Elias tackled them both.

Tug-o-war was simpler. No magic was involved. Brody led the line, Thomas anchored the back, Silas and Elias in the middle. They won again, somehow.

As the boys made their way to the stands, Thomas felt something he hadn't in a long time: freedom. No stress. No survival instincts. Just joy.

Elias later joined a speed spellcasting challenge he won, surprising even Castel's classmates.

Mari and Eva tried enchanted jousting. With magical armor and foot-locked skateboards, they charged each other. Mari flew backward on impact, armor flaring with protective magic. She landed on the mats laughing.

The night continued until the grand finale.

Upperclassmen stepped into the arena to showcase their powers. Blue mages crafted ice sculptures, and red mages melted them. Hybrids began performing dual-colored auras, combining unique effects. One created a blackout illusion. Another summoned fire-infused lightning. Yet another made the grass *dance*.

Then came Castel.

"Introducing our top sophomore Castel!" the announcer declared.

He stepped forward, a red aura crackling from his right hand and blue mist coiling from his left. Fire and water wrapped around each other, spiraling into a glowing orb. The orb grew into a floating mini-sun.

Green aura flowed off Castel's body. Vines rose and danced, petals unfolding with yellow sparks like fireflies. With a dramatic spin, he clapped four auras merging. The orb pulsed and shrank into a glowing seed.

A bolt of lightning struck it. Golden light exploded like fireworks, petals raining gently over the crowd.

Then Castel reached out and pulled the aura back. The seed dissolved in his palm.

Silence.

Then thunderous applause.

"Did he just use *four* disciplines?" Elias shouted.

"I thought two was hard!" Mari exclaimed.

"God-level control," Brody muttered, standing to applaud. "I've never seen past three."

Thomas may not have *seen* the aura, but he'd seen enough.

As the festival ended, the group headed to the dorms. Mari and Eva split off. Thomas made a quick stop at the restroom. As he washed his hands, he overheard two teachers.

"Fun festival, but... did you notice the boy in dodgeball?"

"You mean the auburn-haired one with white in his bangs?"

"Yeah. No aura. Not a trace. Even during Tug-o-war nothing."

Thomas froze.

"Let's go, man! Before the showers fill up!" Elias called, slapping his back.

Thomas nodded and followed, casting a final glance at the teachers.

Do I not possess magic?

The question chilled him to the core.

9

DANTE JR

Yawning, Thomas squinted as the early morning sun broke through the window and landed on his face. With a groan, he rolled over, trying to escape the light, but to no avail. Elias was already up and moving around the dorm room, his every step and clink of his coffee cup sending jolts of overstimulation through Thomas's foggy mind.

Sitting up, Thomas shot Elias a death glare before swinging his legs over the edge of the bed. "You're so loud," he muttered, rubbing his face.

Outside, the excited chatter and footsteps of other students echoed down the hall. It was the first official day of classes at Blackwood. Thomas dressed quickly, the buzz of energy just outside the door making him more anxious.

"Do we have all the same classes today?" he asked Elias, hoping for reassurance.

"Yeah, we do," Elias replied, sipping his coffee.

Music to Thomas's ears.

Suddenly, the door burst open. Brody stormed in with a

grin plastered on his face, grabbed Thomas by the arm, and practically dragged him out of the room. "Let's go! Day one, let's get some grub!" he shouted. Thomas instinctively reached back and yanked Elias along with them.

Silas followed, apparently having arrived at their dorm alongside Brody.

The morning moved fast. They made their way to the cafeteria, grabbing trays of food. Mari and Eva were already seated, though Castel was nowhere in sight. Despite the cheerful atmosphere, there was an undercurrent of nerves. No one really knew what to expect.

Silas bounced his leg anxiously, shaking the table. Elias's coffee swirled in its to-go container. Thomas stared out toward the flood of first-years pouring into the cafeteria and toward their classrooms. The weight of the words he'd overheard the night before *no aura* settled heavily on his chest, his breath catching.

He closed his eyes for a moment and exhaled. Mari and Elias noticed, their expressions softening. Brody, on the other hand, was too busy entertaining Silas and Eva to catch the shift in mood.

"Look who it is the newbies! You all excited for your first day?" Castel's voice broke the tension. Silas stopped shaking, and Thomas lifted his head.

"Aye! There he is we were wondering where you went," Brody beamed, waving him over.

"I was just checking in. Gotta get to my own classes," Castel said, patting Thomas on the shoulder. "If you need anything, let me know."

Thomas offered a grateful smile and nod.

"Remember," Castel added as he turned toward Lee, the

student who had brought Mari to the school, "today's just the first day. Nothing has to go perfectly."

Once he left, the group resumed chatting with everyone except Thomas. His chest still felt tight, and his breathing was shallow like he couldn't quite catch his breath. The feeling lingered as they finished their meals and headed to class.

Their first class was on one of the upper floors with a teacher named Juno Whitmore.

The lecture hall was massive, lined with cushioned seats. The group split into pairs. Thomas and Elias found a spot near the center. Elias set down his books and pencils with practiced ease.

"Can I borrow a pencil?" Thomas asked.

Elias slid one over without looking up.

"Also... paper?"

Elias side-eyed him and sighed, passing over an entire notebook. "Keep it. I've got extras."

Thomas chuckled softly, flipping open the notebook and waiting.

Then, the classroom doors slammed open.

In strode Juno Whitmore, an older woman with white hair, dressed in suit pants and a blazer. She moved like a whirlwind, her steps purposeful and dramatic.

"Welcome! Welcome! Sit, sit!" she bellowed, spinning on her heel with arms flung wide like a performer on stage.

"I am Juno Whitmore, your first obstacle this year!" She clapped her hands, and a red aura flared between her palms, dripping fire. With a snap, it turned blue and transformed into pouring water.

"Everything you do must have purpose, ladies and gentlemen!" she roared. Books floated around her in a swirl of golden aura, a marker scribbling notes on the board behind her.

Her aura shifted again to purple now, her body flickering like it was being fast-forwarded.

"SometimesHybridColorsCauseMultiEffects!" she spoke in a rapid blur. Elias scribbled furiously, every word sacred. Thomas leaned over to copy from his notes.

As the electricity crackled through her aura, she explained, "It's not just about base colors it's about shades, tints. Every hue has a purpose. Just like all of you."

Her smile was dazzling. "Now! One by one, come down and show your aura. Don't just let it flow. Like peeing."

The room erupted in giggles. Brody's laugh echoed loudest.

"She's... a bit much," Thomas whispered.

Elias nodded. "That's for sure."

Students began demonstrating their auras, some flowing with vibrant colors, others dull or incomplete. Elias's was a soft red with subtle flames. Then it was Thomas's turn.

He stepped forward, closed his eyes, and tried. He copied what he had seen and willed his aura to appear. Seconds passed. Nothing.

Peeking, he found the class staring.

"Well? WELL?" Juno demanded, circling him.

"I'm trying," Thomas murmured, cheeks flushed.

A few students snickered. His friends frowned, sympathetic.

Juno sighed, rummaged through her desk, and pulled out a wand. "This'll help for unawakened mages. Use it wisely. It runs on willpower, but it's not permanent. Don't make it a crutch."

She ushered him back to his seat. He could hardly breathe.

Could he really not summon an aura? Could that get him expelled? Should he just pretend everything was fine?

His thoughts spiraled. The walk back felt like a parade

of shame. Snickers followed. His head throbbed. The old headaches returned. His chest tightened, and his ears rang.

Fake mage, fake mage, fake mage.

The words looped like a curse.

He was so close to becoming someone new. But the bullies had found their way back to him.

Elias nudged him gently, snapping him back. The class was ending. Thomas forced himself to stand.

"Hey, it's okay," Elias said softly.

Thomas nodded with a fake smile. "Yeah. It'll be fine."

The lump in his throat said otherwise.

As they headed to their next class, Brody threw in his two cents: "Maybe you're constipated."

Mari, in contrast, was drafting a meal plan and training schedule to help "activate" his aura. Eva chimed in, offering surprisingly accurate advice on strength training.

Fake mage, fake mage! Fake mage!" A kid suddenly shouted, laughing as a few of his goons high-fived him. They chanted it loudly while walking into the classroom with Thomas and the others. Thankfully, most of the other students didn't seem to care much about Thomas's lack of aura apparently, being a late bloomer wasn't all that rare.

"Late bloomers usually awaken in the first couple weeks. The classes and the wand help force it out," Silas said, patting Thomas on the back reassuringly.

The second class was marginally better, but not by much. This time, they were expected to use their actual aura to perform magic, which only made things ten times more awkward for Thomas. Most of the other students stood confidently at the front, lifting objects, breathing fire, and spraying water from their hands. But when it was Thomas's turn, he stood in front of the class with a pained expression on his face.

He pulled out his wand and pointed it toward a set of books. The teachers, likely aware of his situation from some kind of group chat, watched in silent anticipation. Thomas drew in a slow, shaky breath, his eyes squeezing shut. A faint yellow aura finally seeped from the wand, wrapping around the books. They began to lift, but the aura wavered, unstable, the energy quivering before it gave out, and the books crashed onto the table below.

Snickers erupted across the room. The headache returned stronger this time. It felt like Dante all over again. Thomas wanted to hurl something out of sheer frustration.

"Good job, Thomas. That's exactly what we expect from wand users," the teacher said. Maybe it was meant to be encouraging, but it felt like a needle stabbing his chest. How was that supposed to make him feel better?

He slinked back to his seat, now surrounded by his friends, who all tried to lift his spirits. Unlike Blackwood Academy, he actually had friends here, and that small comfort helped ease the throbbing in his skull if only a little.

The rest of the day passed in a similar fashion to students learning about auras, how they worked, and how to harness them. Everything being taught should have been wondrous and exciting. But for Thomas, it was like listening to stories about something invisible he could never touch. With each class, each passing hour, he felt more and more hopeless.

As the school day came to a close, Thomas and his friends made their way to the cafeteria. The group was unusually quiet, all of them feeling the weight of his mood. Elias opened his mouth to say something but was interrupted.

"Look there! It's a fake image!" a boy shouted. It was James

Verling, a pipsqueak who'd been in all of Thomas's classes and had spent the day mocking him. Now that classes were over, his taunts were louder and direct.

"Look at the kid. Can I even *see* auras?" one of James's pig-faced goons sneered.

Thomas didn't reply. He didn't want to give them any more ammunition by looking even more pathetic than he already felt.

"Back off him, piggy!" Brody snapped.

"I didn't know mice and pigs were companions!" Mari added.

Thomas snorted and covered his mouth to hide a smile as both bullies turned red with anger.

"Oh, so that's how you wanna play it?" James growled. But before he could say anything more, a hand landed on Mari's shoulder.

Castel stood behind them, grinning.

"Now, now, Verling. Why don't you run off to your brother? I'm sure he'd love to hear whose bad side you're getting on. Go tell the wet rat about how you're picking fights with *my* friends," Castel said calmly, but the weight behind his words was unmistakable. He'd clearly dealt with the Verlings before.

James clenched his fists, grabbed his goon by the arm, and stormed away.

"Thanks. Today's been... a bitch," Thomas muttered, relieved.

Castel frowned and scratched the back of his head. He knew. Everyone knew. Thomas was the only unawakened student this year, and the rumor had spread like wildfire.

"Hey, it's fine, man. Just take it one day at a time. It's not that uncommon for kids to awaken late," Castel said.

"It's not that he's awakening late," Elias blurted. "He doesn't have an aura at all."

SMACK! Eva's hand, glowing pink, struck Elias across the head.

"Don't rub salt in the wound, four-eyes!" she snapped, hissing.

The group fell silent. None of them had realized Thomas was missing an aura entirely. Thomas himself had been unaware since he couldn't see them.

"What does that mean?" he asked, frowning. Mari looked equally confused.

"It means… you might not be a mage," Elias said quietly.

The words struck Thomas like a blade. *Might not be a mage?* His chest tightened. His vision blurred. He stumbled back a few steps and clutched his abdomen.

"Hey, let's just eat something. No need to stress about this now," Eva said gently, placing a hand on his back.

"I'm… not hungry," Thomas lied. He was starving, but the thought of eating made him feel sick.

He gave a weak, fake smile and waved at them as he backed away. Their sad expressions lingered as he turned and headed toward the dorms, his shoulders weighed down with pressure. His stomach twisted. His mind swirled.

Would Samuel be disappointed in him?

He slipped off his shoes and climbed into bed, still fully dressed. Eyes fixed on the ceiling, he pulled the blanket over himself. The world pulsed softly around him.

When the door creaked open, he assumed it was Elias.

He was wrong.

Standing in the doorway was a decaying version of himself. The corpse-like figure raised a hand, fingers glowing. Thomas opened his mouth to scream, but no sound came. He scrambled backward, heart pounding.

The decayed figure moved closer. Pain exploded through Thomas's body. His bones vibrated. His eyes rolled back. Finally, a blood-curdling scream escaped him.

Agony surged through him like fire. His mouth couldn't form words, only howls of pain. Through the haze, he saw the corpse's fingers flicker with something: a black flame. No... a black aura.

Tears welled in Thomas's eyes as a glowing rune appeared on the decaying figure's exposed bones. He blacked out, his head snapping back onto the pillow.

Then he jolted awake.

Moonlight poured into the room. Elias snored softly across from him. Thomas was panting, drenched in sweat. He sat up, hands roaming over his body.

Tears dripped onto the sheets. Slowly, he collapsed back onto the pillow and stared up at the ceiling.

"What the hell was that?"

10

TIME TO DUEL

Thomas woke up late the next morning, his sheets and pillow damp with sweat again. He really needed to find a place to wash his stuff. As he sat up slowly, his eyes found Elias seated at his desk with a cup of black coffee buried in a book, just like the day before. A strange sense of déjà vu washed over Thomas. It felt like he'd seen this scene a hundred times, even though it had only been three days.

After getting dressed and lacing his shoes, he began his morning routine, which was eerily similar to yesterday's, until the door burst open.

Elias jumped, startled. Brody barged in, eyes bright with excitement, grabbing Thomas by the arm and pulling both him and Elias out the door. Silas followed closely behind.

In the cafeteria, they met Eva and Mari, gathered around one of the round lunch tables. Castel even joined them that morning, and for a while, they joked, laughed, and threw paper scraps at each other. Thomas sat quietly, the memory of his vivid dreams and the wand he'd received yesterday weighing heavily on him. The thought gnawed at him. What if they found out he wasn't a real mage?

"Thomas. Hey." Brody's voice pulled him back. Thomas looked up from his untouched tray to see the others watching him with soft, concerned smiles. His eyes met Brody's.

"You were just... staring at your food," Brody said. "So... can I have it if you're not gonna eat it?"

There was a collective groan.

"It's free! Go get more, you loaf!" Mari shouted, hurling an empty milk carton at him.

"Why would I get more when there's perfectly good food right there?" Brody shot back.

Laughter returned to the table as Brody claimed Thomas's tray, cheering and playfully slapping him on the back, though a little harder than necessary.

"Castel, what classes are you taking right now?" Mari asked, eyes wide with curiosity.

Shoveling a spoonful of oatmeal and fruit into his mouth, Castel smiled as he chewed and swallowed. "Well, I'm a second year student, so I'm learning hybrid magic."

"Why does that matter?" Brody asked with his mouth full of Thomas's food.

"Because each year studies something different," Elias explained.

"First year is basic spells and aura control. Second year is hybrid magic. Third year covers artifacts, personal weapons, and physical combat. Fourth year is about high-tier spells and unique magical paths," Castel continued.

"So... we never learn basic stuff like math and science?" Mari asked, sounding slightly disappointed.

"Oh, you do," Castel said. "It's just spread out across the year. And in the mage world, it's easier to enhance your basic knowledge through aura absorption. That's a fourth-year skill."

They paused. Mari tilted her head.

"It's... the ability to absorb knowledge from non-magical books," Castel clarified.

"How does it know if a book isn't magical?" Thomas asked, raising an eyebrow.

"When a mage writes about magic, their aura seeps into the pages. That aura forms a barrier, keeping other mages from absorbing the knowledge unfairly."

Everyone nodded like it made perfect sense. Maybe they were used to the logic of magic.

"Can't a mage suppress their aura while writing, then?" Thomas pressed. "So someone could absorb magical knowledge without the aura barrier?"

Castel grinned like Thomas had asked the golden question.

"That's exactly the kind of curiosity you need," he said, winking. Then, standing and saluting with two fingers, he added, "Class starts soon. Don't be late."

As he walked away, his words echoed in Thomas's head. *That's the kind of curiosity you need.* Was he trying to tell him something?

Before Thomas could ponder it further, everyone gathered their things. He followed behind as they made their way to class.

Their morning class was with Magnus Vale, a towering, battle-scarred woman who taught defense and reaction time. Her booming voice commanded the space.

"You focus your aura, you can break anyone's offense!" she barked. Slamming her fists together, a swirl of pink energy flared around her as the ground cracked beneath her.

But Thomas wasn't focused. He leaned back on his hands in

the grass, watching with numb detachment. He felt like none of this mattered. Not if he didn't belong here.

He could feel James's gaze, sharp and hot, on his skin. Castel's words hadn't ended the bullying. Thomas took a deep breath, his chest heavy with frustration.

"I'm going to pair you up randomly!" Magnus bellowed. "Time to duel. Friendly sparring. Try not to kill each other!"

Thomas silently prayed to be paired with a friend. Elias would be ideal.

"You there. Over there," she pointed.

Thomas turned to see his opponent, Gerald. He wasn't James. In fact, Gerald had never called him a fake mage. That in itself felt strange.

Magnus walked between the students. "First rule: no killing. Second rule: don't die. Go!"

The duels erupted, sending fire, water, and lightning flashing through the air. Magnus's eyes were closed, but her powerful aura blanketed the field, monitoring everything.

"Hey, look," Thomas said, raising his wand. "All I've got is this."

Before he could finish, his muscles seized. His body convulsed, and he hit the dirt, groaning. Gerald had used his aura to tase him.

Thomas gripped the wand as a stray blast fired from its tip, breaking the stun. He panted, still tingling, rising unsteadily. *How do I survive this?*

Gerald slammed his aura into Thomas's gut. He gasped, spitting into the dirt, pain radiating through him.

Then visions.

He saw Dante's decaying corpse. His lifeless self beside it. His body trembled, fury rising. *Why now? What was this?* His head slammed into the ground again. He looked up to find his teacher giving him a side-eye.

"*Bitch.*" The word distorted in his head. His face burned red.

Digging into the dirt, Thomas pushed himself up. "Yellow," he whispered.

A yellow aura flickered to life, curling toward him like a shadow. It formed a glowing fist and swung down. Thomas stepped aside just in time.

Now he saw its colors: red, blue, pink, and yellow from nearby students. He looked at his wand. A red blast shot out fire.

Gerald dodged, countering with water. The fire sizzled out.

Thomas grinned. *It's on.*

Gerald charged.

Thomas fired a pink aura around himself just as Gerald's punch connected. The hit landed solid, but Thomas didn't flinch. The pink aura held him firm.

Their eyes locked.

Thomas reeled back to punch, but Magnus's voice thundered. "ALRIGHT, duels over!"

Everything stopped. Gerald's aura faded. So did Thomas's.

They returned to their groups. Silas was scuffed, Elias and Eva looked untouched, and Mari and Brody had some dirt on them but clearly held their own.

Thomas figured he fell in with Silas, scuffed up and probably on the losing end.

As they chatted, Brody recounted his brawl, Mari boasted her cleverness, and Elias and Eva remained modestly quiet.

Silas said nothing. Thomas stepped beside him and clapped his shoulder. "Next time."

Silas smiled gently, nodding.

"How was your duel, Thomas?" Eva asked with a bright smile.

He blushed, rubbing the back of his head.

"I... I can see the aura."

Silence. Then shouts and hugs.

Eva's embrace nearly crushed him. Brody cheered, Mari laughed, and even Elias cracked a grin.

"Next step: unlock your aura and destroy everyone," Brody grinned.

"Maybe it's stress-related?" Mari mused.

"If it were, he'd have unlocked it already," Elias replied.

They continued debating the cause while Thomas quietly basked in the warmth of their joy.

He was happy, but a thought nagged him.

Why did I see Dante? Why my own corpse?

He considered telling them. But for now, he just wanted to enjoy the moment. To accept the love he'd been given.

11

ANIMAL FARM

It had been a few months since Thomas had unlocked the ability to see auras. The problem was he hadn't made any progress since. While his grades remained decent, and he could wield his wand well enough to pass tests, it was becoming increasingly stressful. He felt stuck, and everyone else seemed to feel it too.

Students began to distance themselves, treating him like a fluke. Most assumed he wouldn't last until the end of the year, so they didn't bother trying to get close. The teachers weren't much better. Many had started ignoring him altogether as if seeing auras no longer made him worth their time. To them, he was a drain on space, on effort, on resources.

His friends tried to keep his spirits up, but Thomas sensed their faith wavering. Castel and Elias were the only ones who never doubted him. Brody still held onto hope, but the excitement he'd once shown had dulled. Silas remained quiet, as always. Mari had stopped brainstorming ways to help him awaken his magic. They hadn't abandoned him but they didn't seem to know what was coming.

That day's magical biology class was different; they were visiting the academy's farm. Thomas moved slower than usual, relying heavily on his wand for support. What felt like a temporary crutch was beginning to feel permanent. Practicing aura color shifting wore him out more than ever, the mental toll leaving him drained.

Their class moved through the sprawling barn and glass enclosure to the other side. Eva stuck close to him. She was becoming a good friend. Best of all, Castel was part of the class that day, and Thomas had been waiting for a chance to see him in action as a mage instructor rather than just a fellow student. Castel pointed out different magical creatures, explaining how they mirrored animals found in human zoos except with arcane properties. According to him, magical creatures did exist in the human world too. "Closed minds miss out on a lot," he said, locking eyes with Thomas. Thomas quickly looked away.

"You okay?" Eva leaned over and asked quietly.

"Yeah, I'm fine."

"You sure? You look a little... blah."

"Blah's a good word for it. Just tired."

"Don't overdo it, okay?"

Before he could respond, Elias interrupted. "Guys, listen."

Thomas and Eva turned their attention back to Castel, who had resumed speaking while subtly keeping an eye on them. The group exited the barn into a massive open field, where older students from the Summoner's Club were tending to the animals. Their club duties included magical animal care.

Silas looked like he was in heaven, practically bouncing on his toes.

Huge geckos sprinted across the grass toward the forest. Deer with glowing, oversized antlers grazed peacefully. Fire sprites, small red orbs with legs, darted about like living embers. They couldn't burn anything, but they *felt* like they could.

Mari stood at the front, inching closer to Castel every time he stopped to speak.

"You know, she's not subtle," Thomas whispered to Eva.

"Yeah," Eva smirked. "But I don't even think she knows how she feels about him."

They laughed softly, the moment feeling oddly normal.

"Go ahead and explore!" Castel announced. The students scattered.

Thomas wandered to a wooden fence, resting against it as he watched the magical creatures. Then it happened.

"Fake mage!" James's voice rang out.

Thomas flinched. He stared straight ahead, trying to ignore him. He wished he had the energy to defend himself, but he was used to it now. Teachers skipped him when he raised his hand. Rumors swirled that the faculty wanted him gone. Some believed he wasn't a true mage at all, just a human infiltrator.

It sounded absurd, but Elias had once told him about a brutal mage-versus-human war that happened long before firearms existed. "Human will may be stronger than magic," Elias had said.

The words echoed in Thomas's mind. *If I'm human... is that why I'm still here? Is that why I haven't given up?*

He was so deep in thought he didn't notice the floating koi fish approaching. The creature drifted down to meet him at eye level. Quietly, Thomas reached out and stroked its shimmering scales, awe softening his features. The class noticed and rushed over, startling it. The fish flitted skyward, fleeing.

"They're skittish," Castel explained, "and they rarely approach anyone uninvited."

89

"Why'd that thing get so close to *him?*" James sneered. "Maybe it sensed he has *no* aura!"

James's goon howled with laughter, Gerald smirking before walking off.

"Or maybe it sensed his *brain*," Eva shot back, striding up beside Thomas. "Guess that's why they avoid you."

Thomas grinned. "Yeah, that explains it."

James turned red, fists clenched. "Don't you *dare* act smug! I'll wipe that look off your face!"

Thomas reached for his wand.

"I'll crush that thing with my aura!" James growled.

Suddenly, Castel clapped hard. A wave of force knocked James, his lackey, Thomas, and Eva into the fence. Thomas caught Eva by the wrist, steadying her.

"You okay?" he asked.

She nodded, blushing slightly.

"No fighting," Castel warned. "Not in class, not outside a sanctioned duel. If you want to spar, do it the right way."

Thomas nodded silently. Castel gave him an apologetic look.

"Sorry, Thomas. I can't pick sides."

"It's fine," Thomas said softly. Castel gave him a reassuring pat and turned away.

Thomas's gaze followed him and then froze.

Decay and Dante. The spectral, decaying visions of himself. Dante's jawless grin. Decay's black-glowing fingertips. He could smell them rot and death. Their presence was stronger now, almost real.

A ringing filled his ears. He couldn't hear anything else. Just the corpses.

Eva stepped into view, cutting off his line of sight.

"Thomas? Hey, are you okay?" she asked, her voice worried.

He blinked and looked into her eyes. He exhaled sharply. He'd been holding his breath.

"Yeah. Yeah, I'm good," he whispered.

The koi fish returned, floating before him like a gentle specter. It hovered behind the barrier as if it recognized him.

As the sun dipped below the horizon, Thomas sat on a bench near the farm. The fish lingered nearby, watching him like an old friend.

Castel sat beside him, one arm resting along the back of the bench.

"The others wanted me to check on you. Said you've been out of it all day."

Thomas didn't answer right away.

"I told Eva and Elias I was fine. Just needed to think," he said, his tone sharper than intended.

He glanced sideways. Decay and Dante were still there.

"You know, there's a legend about koi fish," Castel said, brushing past the tension. "They say flying koi can sense familiar auras past, present, or future."

Thomas raised an eyebrow.

"They also respond to something called *pure aura.*"

Pure aura? The words echoed in his head.

"Maybe you're looking at it all the wrong way," Castel said.

Thomas snapped. "Then tell me, what's the *right* way?"

"Shh," Castel said gently, placing a hand on Thomas's back. It was warm. Familiar. Comforting.

Thomas's eyes welled up. "Sorry," he whispered.

"Don't force it," Castel said. "Just have faith."

"It's hard," Thomas admitted.

"It'll get harder. But don't stop fighting. Keep using your wand. Don't give up."

Thomas didn't know how to respond. He glanced at Decay, who was staring at Castel now. Did Castel see them too?

"Fine," Thomas said, guarded.

Castel stood and placed a hand on his shoulder. "It'll be okay."

Then he left.

Thomas closed his eyes, leaning back. *Will it really be okay?*

He felt himself falling into another dream.

The farm, daylight. Castel teaching. James beside him.

"Can you train me with hybrid magic?" James asked.

Of course, man. That's what friends are for. The words left Thomas's mouth unbidden.

Aura flickered from his hand changing colors, settling on violet.

A memory? A dream?

Suddenly, Decay's hands clutched his face. A black aura oozed into his skull. Bones rattled.

Thomas screamed.

He hit the ground, coughing, crying, clawing at the dirt. *What's happening to me?*

12

AURA AURA

Thomas woke the next morning exhausted as if he hadn't slept at all. Sitting up in bed, he moved through his routine like clockwork. Right on cue, Brody burst through the door with his usual boundless energy and excitement, same as yesterday, same as the day before. It made Thomas wonder if the kid was chugging energy drinks at sunrise.

The morning unfolded like any other. The four of them made their way to the cafeteria, joining Mari and Eva. But something was off. Thomas's head throbbed, his eyes burned, and a strange ache settled deep in his bones like they were on fire. It made the nightmares from the night before all the more disturbing.

There was another oddity: Castel had joined them for breakfast, laughing and chatting with the group. Thomas, however, could hardly register the words. His body felt sick like it was trying to reject itself. Not far from their table sat James, his presence needling at Thomas's nerves. Whispers floated across the cafeteria. "Fake Mage," repeated like a chant. The weight of those words settled in Thomas's gut like a stone.

"You okay, Thomas?" Eva asked. He looked up from his tray to find everyone staring at him. He forced a weak smile and gave a thumbs-up.

"Oh yeah, of course."

His voice was bright, but the unease twisted beneath his skin.

Conversations resumed, none of them involving Thomas. When they finished eating, the group headed off to class. Thomas stayed behind, muttering something about forgetting his wand. The lie stung his throat it always did. He was the only student who actually needed one.

Back in his dorm, he sat on the edge of his bed, staring at the doorway. That same doorway where, months ago, he'd first seen the decaying corpse from his dreams. What did it mean? That dream, that *memory*, they were blurring together. Seeing his own dead body had felt like a premonition, one he couldn't shake. Clutching his wand, he left for class, just making it before the bell rang.

He took an empty seat and leaned back, ignoring the kid next to him, who was already recoiling in disgust. *Fake Mage.* That label haunted every hallway, every classroom.

"Alright, let's make this quick," the teacher announced, stepping onto the central platform in the auditorium. The room was shaped like a stadium, with seats rising around a tall, vaulted space.

With a clap and a flick of his wrist, the teacher summoned towering stone runes. "Today we're learning about Color Shifting. But instead of a boring lecture... you're going to earn your A." He began pacing. "First five to reach the top platform win. No rules. Go."

The runes lit up instantly. No one really knew what to do

except Brody, of course. He launched from his seat, targeting the nearest glowing yellow rune. But the moment his feet touched it, the rune pulsed violently, slinging him backward into the crowd.

"Brody, are you okay?" Silas called, rushing to him. Brody raised a shaky thumbs-up.

While the class hesitated, Elias stepped forward. He found a red rune, matched its aura, and calmly rose upward on the platform. That set everything into motion. Students explored with colorful auras, leaping from rune to rune.

Thomas froze.

He didn't have an aura. Panic bubbled up. He was going to fail. Laughter echoed from above.

"Fake Mage! Enjoy the F!" James jeered.

Whether it was embarrassment, rage, or raw teenage defiance, Thomas yanked out his wand.

If I can't make an aura, I'll force one.

He leaped from his desk toward an unclaimed yellow rune. Channeling magic through his wand, he fired. The rune sparked violently, but he landed. It was held. The platform surged upward.

As it climbed, the rune shifted from yellow to red. Thomas twisted his wand, adjusting the aura. Flames crackled from its tip. He was adapting to climbing.

Mari navigated the course with calculated precision, sticking to warm color transitions. Elias was a blur, his control unmatched. Silas and Eva were mid-pack. Brody, with his single-color focus, was being hurled like a rag doll.

Thomas was closing in on Elias when a blast hit his chest, sending him flying.

Thomas crashed onto a random platform, bounced off, and

barely managed to catch a blue one with his wand. Gritting his teeth, he stood and retaliated. Blue magic clashed with yellow as he struck James's platform. Sparks flew. The platform collapsed, sending James and his friend tumbling.

Chaos erupted.

Three platforms shattered, and several students dropped. The trampoline-like floor saved them from serious injury, but the damage was done.

Thomas wasn't in the top five. He was seventh.

As the platforms descended and class ended, the teacher offered no praise, only a cold glance. Thomas clenched his jaw, trying to ignore James's next outburst.

"He cheated! He used his wand! He doesn't even have an aura!"

Whispers surged around him. *Cheater. Fake mage. Now, a cheating mage.*

Thomas wanted to defend himself, but the destruction, the hurt students, Brody's unfinished climb, it was too much.

He clenched his wand, rage boiling under his skin. This was supposed to be his way out. His chance. But it was slipping away.

Then came the voice.

Show them all.

Cold fingers gripped his shoulder. Decay. Closer than ever. Cheek to cheek.

Prove what you can do. DO IT!

Thomas screamed, collapsing. Elias and Eva caught him.

He awoke to gentle thumps and morning light. Sitting up in bed, he blinked. James was sleeping across from him.

What?

The room was... different. Posters on the walls. Photos. His desk was neat. Clothes he'd never seen before. Expensive ones.

My hair...

Short, clean, styled. His teeth were white. His skin was clear. He looked... good.

He stared at his reflection in awe, then fear.

"What are you doing?" James murmured.

"Nothing. Nightmare," Thomas muttered, brushing it off. But his aura pulsed naturally now. He could control it. Shift it.

Panicked, he bolted to Elias's room. A ward tried to stop him, but he pushed through.

Elias spun around. "How did you break my ward?!"

"Elias, it's me! Thomas!"

"I *know* who you are. Why are you here?" Elias snapped. "We told you to leave us alone!"

Thomas flinched. "No, Elias, you don't understand."

"GET OUT!"

Shaken, Thomas ran to find Castel.

"Castel!" he cried.

"Uh, yeah?" Castel said, clearly confused. Eva and Lee shrugged.

"You don't remember me?" Thomas pleaded. "You found me! At the orphanage!"

But Castel just stared, puzzled. "Sorry, kid. Who are you again?"

Thomas broke. Tears spilled down his face as the world slowed. Froze.

Then, the burning began.

Bones vibrated. Stomach twisted. Vomit hit the pavement.

Thomas collapsed, screaming.

He woke up screaming.

Eva and Elias held him down, calming him. Sweat poured off

him. Students whispered around the room. The teacher didn't even look up.

Elias and Eva took him to his dorm. He skipped the rest of the day.

The pain was worse now. The dreams unbearable. His trust narrowed to two people, Elias and Eva. Soon, he would have to tell them everything.

CHAPTER 13

13

Chapter 13

The weekend finally arrived, offering a much-needed breath of peace. Thomas sat quietly in the common room, sipping a smoothie while flipping through a thick book titled *Auras: The History of Awakening*. It was a dense, medical-style text on mages who experienced their aura awakening later in life. It was not exactly a page-turner, which was why the smoothie helped make the experience a little more bearable.

Around him, a handful of students lounged. Some were immersed in video games, and others were watching funny clips online. As Thomas turned another page, he spotted Elias out of the corner of his eye. He raised his smoothie in greeting. Elias strolled over and plopped down beside him.

"What's up?" Elias asked, raising a brow.

Thomas held up the book. "Trying to understand my body."

An awkward pause settled between them.

"The aura part of me," Thomas waved vaguely. "You know what? Forget it."

Elias chuckled. "Well, besides self-discovery, learning anything new?"

"Only that I'm broken."

"Broken mage," Elias corrected.

"I wouldn't even call myself that."

"Then I'll do it for you. Someone's got to keep the faith."

"Thanks," Thomas said with a faint smile. He leaned on his knuckles and closed the book. "Hey... can I tell you something? It's kind of important."

Elias nodded, expression softening. Thomas took a slow breath.

"I'm seeing... a dead version of myself."

The words hit the air heavily. Despite the chatter in the room, it felt like everything else had gone silent. Thomas glanced sideways, searching Elias's face for a reaction.

Elias looked rattled but thoughtful. "Let's head back to the dorm. I want to test something."

Thomas nodded, deciding to trust him. They exited the foyer and walked through the mostly empty halls. Most students were off exploring campus or enjoying hobbies, making the corridors unusually quiet.

As they turned a corner, a hand suddenly yanked Thomas by the collar and slammed him against the wall.

It was James flanked by his goon, Preston (nicknamed "Piggy"). James's face was twisted in fury.

"I know what you did, cheater!" he spat. "You fake mages think you can just *cheat* your way through and ruin it for the rest of us? Try that again and I'll make you regret it!"

James jabbed a finger at Thomas's face. His voice echoed, growing louder in Thomas's ringing ears.

"He looked like he was coming for you!" Piggy snarled, using it as an excuse to grab Elias and slam him into the wall. "Four-eyes needs to learn his place too!"

Rage surged in Thomas. His heart thundered. His eyes locked on James's finger.

"Oh yeah?" James sneered. "Then let me remind you, if you don't disappear, I'll make your life HELL!"

Piggy reached for Elias's glasses.

Then CRACK.

James hadn't realized his grip on Thomas's collar had loosened. It was just enough for Thomas to get out of his grip.

Thomas's head slammed into Piggy's nose with a sickening crunch. Blood sprayed. Piggy staggered back, clutching his face, wailing in pain.

"Dude! He's a psycho!" James screamed, backing away in horror. Piggy's face was already swelling and darkening with bruises. Blood poured between his fingers.

"Let's go!" James shouted, dragging his friend down the hallway.

Silence returned to the corridor. Elias leaned against the wall, stunned. The two boys exchanged glances, then walked in silence back toward their dorm.

They didn't speak, but both knew the truth: this incident wouldn't stay between them. And it didn't.

Whispers raced through the school like wildfire, and each retelling twisted the facts further.

Across campus, Brody trained in a field while Silas studied magical creatures nearby.

Brody was focused, aura flickering around him in golden hues. He closed his eyes, trying to overlay a faint purple tint. The colors clashed, yellow wrapping his body while purple attempted to bind on top. His right arm began to twist, claws forming as his skin stretched and warped.

"Come on, come on…" he muttered through clenched teeth.

Then BANG.

The two layers of aura violently rejected one another, sparks flying as Brody was blasted across the field. He landed hard, his breath knocked from his lungs and stared up at the clouds.

For a long time, Brody had felt something dark creeping in. He'd once been at the top of his class. Now, he was falling behind, barely scraping through assignments. Thomas, even without an aura, was outpacing him.

Jealousy festered.

Only Silas still showed interest in him, and that made the guilt worse.

"You okay?" Silas asked gently, summoning staff in hand. He sat beside Brody and stared at the sky.

Brody forced a smile. "Yeah... Still no successful transmutation."

Silas frowned, hands digging into the dirt. "It's a hard technique. We're only first-years. You'll get there."

Brody nodded, but the lie clung to his tongue. "Yeah... it'll be okay."

He didn't believe it.

Back on campus, Lee jogged toward them, out of breath.

"Did you hear?" he blurted. "Thomas *decked* Piggy broke his nose! Blood everywhere!"

"No way," Brody said, brows rising. "Why?"

"Some old beef, I guess. Nothing new happened today. The teachers are livid, but the headmaster's staying silent."

Brody clenched his jaw. Why *wasn't* Thomas ever held accountable?

"Well... good for him," he said hollowly. The words felt fake. Maybe part of him *wanted* Thomas to face the consequences.

Mari and Eva were buried in books in the library. Mari scoured through history texts and ancient scrolls.

"Why does the Algernon story just stop after Klayde?" she muttered.

Eva leaned in. "What's it say about him?"

"His father kidnapped a royal princess. Then his half-brother died in a duel. His oldest brother came home... then nothing. It just stops."

Eva frowned, flipping through her book. "That's weird."

A nearby student leaned in and whispered in Eva's ear. Her eyes widened.

"No way!" she gasped, drawing shushing noises from others. "Thomas *punched* that fat kid who's always with James!"

"What?" Mari asked, startled.

"They say he attacked him from behind and broke his nose so bad you could see bone."

Mari's expression turned serious. "Don't defend him too quickly, Eva. Physical violence... doesn't just heal."

Eva stayed quiet.

Later, the girls sat with Brody and Silas in the cafeteria.

"Do you think Thomas will actually awaken?" Mari asked suddenly.

"Of course!" Eva replied quickly, but her desperation was obvious. The others were silent.

Then, a voice behind them spoke.

"He will."

It was Elias. Thomas stood beside him, holding a tray of food, face pale. He'd heard them. Heard their doubts.

Only Eva and Elias still believed.

Without a word, he turned and left.

Elias set the tray down. "Thomas might be strange, an aura-seer with no visible aura, but there's a reason. I believe in that."

He left, too, leaving the food untouched.

Back in their moonlit dorm, Thomas and Elias sat on the floor.

"If Decay is real," Elias said quietly, "and only shows himself to you... maybe I can see him through your eyes."

He handed Thomas his glasses. "They're magical lenses. They let me see what you see."

Thomas hesitated, then slowly put them on.

"Fine. But I don't know if he'll show up."

A silence stretched. Then Elias blinked, eyes widening.

"There," Thomas whispered.

"I see him too."

Decay emerged from the shadows. He extended a black-flamed finger toward Elias.

Thomas moved to stop him, but Elias grabbed his wrist. "Don't. I want to see what happens."

Decay touched Elias's skull.

Elias screamed.

The sound was inhuman. His body shook as the pain wracked him. The purple ward over the dorm door glowed violently.

Thomas yanked the glasses off, holding Elias as he collapsed.

"What did you do?!" he screamed at Decay.

Elias, pale and gasping, looked up at Thomas.

"I see him," he whispered.

Thomas held him tighter, tears in his eyes.

"I'm not crazy," he said, laughing through the sobs.

14

TWO OF A KIND

In the days following the fight, the group felt a quiet divide. Thomas and Elias kept mostly to themselves, spending the week training together in isolation. Occasionally, Elias was seen carrying two food trays back to the dormitory, but Thomas never joined the others during meals, only appearing in classes. The rest of the gang stuck to their usual routine, laughing, eating, and hanging out. They even created a group chat and added Elias, hoping he was relaying messages to Thomas, who didn't have a phone.

To lighten the mood, they planned a trip to the upcoming championship sporting event, Aura Clash, a kind of magical paintball and a beloved pastime among mages. The sport resembled traditional human games but cranked up in intensity. It took place in a massive coliseum with two twelve-player teams, randomly assigned to red or blue. The battlefield was a rugged mountain forest, and the goal was to eliminate the enemy team using concentrated aura blasts.

A shimmering magical barrier around the stands ensured spectator safety, allowing an unobstructed view of the chaos below. The barrier highlighted each player's position, lending the game a futuristic, video-game feel.

Castel strolled over with two hot dogs in hand, plopping down beside Mari. Brody and Silas were chatting with Eva a few rows away. As for Elias and Thomas, they hadn't responded to the group's invitation.

Mari took one of the hot dogs, smiling as she bit into it. "I don't think I've seen you this excited in a while, Castel."

Castel smirked, clapping as a player was knocked out. "What can I say? I love a good Aura Clash. During summer breaks in the human world, I binge paintball tournaments. It scratches the same itch."

They watched the game for a few minutes, Castel occasionally jumping to his feet to cheer with the crowd. Still, his eyes kept drifting toward the VIP boxes high above the stands. Though the windows were tinted, he could see straight through them.

"Thinking about being up there one day?" Mari teased, catching his gaze.

"I wouldn't go that far," he replied, eyes still locked on the boxes. "Just... checking them out."

"'Checking them out'? You've been dramatically eyeing them all game."

"You think I'm *dramatically* eyeing some windows?"

Mari gave him a knowing smirk. "I think you're dramatic in everything you do."

Castel chuckled. "Fine, fine." He raised his hands in surrender. "They say some of the most important people in the magical world sit in those boxes."

"Like high-ranking mages?"

He shook his head. "No. I mean the ones you'll probably *never* hear about."

Before Mari could press him further, a loud cheer brought their attention back to the field.

"They're so gonna win," Castel blurted out mid-bite.

Mari raised an eyebrow. "How can you tell?"

Grinning, he pointed to a player highlighted on the battlefield. "That guy, his reaction time's lagging. His team's aura output is weakening. They're almost drained."

He shifted his finger to another figure. "And her? The one with the red and blue hair? She's about to unleash a storm. That'll give her team the edge."

Mari was about to argue, but just then, the exact sequence unfolded. The first player faltered, too slow to react, and was struck hard by a blast, eliminated from the game.

"How do you do that?" Mari asked, stunned.

"What can I say? I observe."

"Or maybe you can read auras better than most."

Castel shrugged. "Maybe I just notice the things others overlook."

Mari went quiet, tapping her foot against the floor. "Can I ask you something?"

He glanced her way, giving her a silent nod.

"Do you think Thomas will awaken?"

His answer came without hesitation. "Yeah. He will."

"What do you know that we don't?"

"Why do you assume I know something?"

"Because you always *do*. It's *annoying!*"

Castel laughed, and Mari blushed as she smiled in spite of herself.

"I *want* to believe Thomas has something special," she

admitted, "but it's not easy for me, not like it is for you or Eva or Elias."

Castel leaned back, folding his arms. "Maybe you don't have to. Not everyone you meet is someone you're destined to believe in right away. Make them *earn* it. Make *him* earn it."

Mari sighed, leaning her head back. "What if he doesn't?"

"Let's talk about the koi fish."

She blinked. "What?"

"Just listen. That koi fish that follows him it's not a coincidence. Koi recognizes aura. Maybe Thomas isn't aura-less. Maybe something's preventing it from showing."

His words sank in slowly, Mari falling silent as her fingers fidgeted in her lap.

"You think he's special?"

"I think he's different. And we all know that."

"That doesn't mean he's special."

"No. But it *means something.* That fish *recognized* him."

He looked at her then, resting a hand on her knee. Her face flushed red.

"There are things we've lost, Mari, ancient knowledge buried from us."

His words lingered. Mari's eyes drifted back to the VIP boxes, a chill running down her spine. She suddenly felt watched, like the game wasn't the only thing under surveillance.

Later, as the event ended and the group started to part ways, Castel vanished quickly, too quickly, like he was chasing someone. Mari told Eva she'd catch up, using the bathroom as an excuse.

She did enter the bathroom but with a different plan. Inside a stall, she leaned her head against the door and took a long, steadying breath. A soft orange circle began to glow around the stall's edges, her portal magic forming. She couldn't teleport inside the VIP room, but she *could* teleport to the window.

Her body shimmered with a grey aura, dissolving into mist. Like smoke, she slid through the cracks around the window, reassembling inside the VIP suite. The portal closed behind her, the smoke fading.

The room was luxurious: leather couches, polished tables, trays of untouched sushi and coffee. But it was empty. The scent of cigar smoke lingered in the air. Along one wall stood a row of aged lockers, each with a name: *Mobius. Olivia. Uma. Thalia. Harper.*

M.O.U.T.H.

Mari hovered her fingers over the names, thinking. *If these really are powerful mages, then forcing the locks would trigger alarms.*

Her gaze shifted to the centerpiece of the room: a dry and silent stone fountain. At its center was a carved phoenix with its mouth open as if frozen mid-cry. Peering in, Mari spotted something: a worn, dust-covered ring.

She reached in and pulled it free.

The gold was dulled by time. The signet was a broken hourglass. Around the band, a partial eclipse was carved in miniature detail.

She stared at it, unmoving. Her eyes welled with tears.

"Dad?" she whispered.

15

DREAMWALKER

"No."

"Yes."

"Elias, I said no."

"Thomas, I said yes!"

The two of them had been arguing all night about Elias's latest idea to dream walk into Thomas's mind and force out the nightmares, so they could finally uncover what was happening together.

"Decay used void magic on you and now me," Elias said, scribbling strange words on a scrap of paper. "Void magic is *illegal*," he stressed, shooting Thomas a serious look. "That means if Decay is you, you've got something illegal inside of you. Void magic can erase anything from existence... even aura."

That silenced Thomas. He began pacing, arms crossed tightly across his chest. It had been a week since Elias last saw Decay, and he'd spent every free moment since studying obsessing. Decay was the first magical phenomenon Elias didn't understand, and that mystery only made him more determined.

But unraveling it meant dragging Thomas into the center of it all.

Thomas groaned, tapping his foot in frustration. "Fine! Fine," he said, at last, deflating as he ran his fingers through his hair. "Just make sure you have a way out. Don't linger. And for the love of everything sacred, do *not snoop*."

Elias raised a brow. "Don't worry, I won't go digging through your nightmares or your fantasies about dating Eva."

Thomas's face turned bright red as he punched Elias in the arm. "Hey! I do *not* have feelings for Eva!"

Elias rolled his eyes. "Sure. Whatever you say."

A few more minutes passed in silence as Elias finished writing. Then, to Thomas's horror, Elias folded the paper and swallowed it.

"Why the hell would you do that?" Thomas asked, rubbing his temples in disbelief.

"It'll protect me until I pass it. Two or three days, tops."

"That won't dissolve in stomach acid?"

Elias frowned. "It'd be easier if it did."

With a shared glance, they both lay down side by side on the floor.

"You ready?" Elias asked.

Thomas exhaled slowly. "Yeah."

Elias reached out and touched Thomas's forehead. A soft purple aura bloomed around his hand, then flowed outward to envelop them both. Their eyes rolled back, bodies going limp. The last thing Thomas heard was Elias's voice:

"Let's see what's really going on in that head of yours."

The ground was scorched. The acrid scent of copper, iron, burnt flesh, and steel filled the air. He'd been here before.

This dream always felt more like a premonition that had

haunted him until he came to the school.

Thomas looked around the battlefield, now a vast, ruined wasteland. Strange symbols were scrawled in ash and fire, and unfamiliar faces lay frozen in death. But Elias was nowhere to be found.

Did he fail to enter the dream?

Thomas began trudging through the carnage, limbs heavy as lead. He glanced down. His hands were caked in dried blood. His aura, once vibrant, flickered weakly drained.

A rumble rippled through the ground. In the distance, through smoke and flame, a small explosion lit the sky.

Clutching his chest, he felt something hard in his pocket. Pulling it out, he found a golden pocket watch. It felt... *familiar,* like something he'd carried his whole life.

"Thomas!"

The voice came from behind him. Turning, Thomas saw Elias older, bloodied, and missing an arm. His face was leaner, his glasses cracked and broken.

"Elias!" Thomas shouted, limping toward him. He caught the stumbling boy, and both collapsed to the ground.

"Elias, we did it, we made it into a dream. What happened to you?"

Elias coughed, blood dribbling from his lips. His eyes had dulled.

"Dream? Ha..." he rasped. "So that's what you meant." His hand grasped Thomas's.

"Don't... stop... trying," he whispered before going still in Thomas's arms.

Suddenly, something hooked into Thomas, wrenching his spirit from his body. He screamed silently as the world twisted around him. A vortex of darkness swallowed everything until he slammed into Elias.

Elias looked normal again.

"What the hell was that?!" Thomas shouted, patting himself down in panic.

"I don't know what you saw, man. I ended up somewhere totally different," Elias said, shaken.

"How?" Thomas asked.

Elias looked away, troubled and uncertain.

They stood in silence, surrounded by blackness.

Thomas swallowed hard. "Do you... want to keep going?"

Elias nodded, more determined than ever. "More than ever."

They clasped hands, their eyes closing. The black void shifted and reformed stone by stone, brick by brick, into a crumbling temple.

When Thomas opened his eyes again, they stood beneath tall, crumbling pillars. Viking runes were etched into the stone walls. Shattered benches lay broken on the floor. It was familiar, but he couldn't place it.

Then a man rushed in, dressed in a sleek black suit, cradling a small child wrapped in a threadbare blanket. He laid the boy on a sacrificial altar.

"That's me," Thomas whispered.

Elias looked at the boy, red-haired, frail, unconscious.

They leaned closer, trying to glimpse the man's face, but it was blurred, unrecognizable.

Then, the man placed his hands on the child's chest. A black aura swirled around him, and his bones glowed beneath his skin. The man chanted in a language neither of them understood.

"He's placing a ward inside you," Elias whispered.

Thomas looked down at his hands. A strange numbness crept over him.

The child screamed, body convulsing. "It hurts! IT HURTS! I'M ON FIRE!"

Thomas stepped back in horror. "It *did* hurt," he muttered. "It felt like... someone was carving into my bones."

Suddenly, Decay burst from behind the man, jaw missing, arm stretched toward Thomas.

"Forget!" it shrieked.

Thomas raised his arms to shield himself, but a blast of energy hit Decay from the side, sending it skidding across the temple floor.

Elias's hands crackled with energy. "Thomas, we have to wake up. *Now!*"

Elias grabbed his collar and yanked him backward. Thomas wanted to fight, to stay, to understand but there was no time. They were dragged out of the temple, up through layers of darkness

and landed flat on the dormitory floor. Morning light poured through the window.

Thomas lay panting, soaked in sweat. "That was *awful*," he groaned.

Elias stood slowly, hands on hips, eyes shut. "That was more than awful. That was... eye-opening."

Thomas stared at him. "Eye-opening? That was *terrifying*."

Elias raised his hands. "I know, I know, but hear me out." He paused. "I think that man carved a ward into your bones. Like, physically *engraved* it into you."

The room went still.

"If that's true... then maybe I *do* have an aura," Thomas whispered, wondering, lighting up his face.

Elias's expression lit up. "You might actually have an aura!"

Thomas grinned. "I have an aura!" he shouted, overjoyed.

"You have an aura!" Elias shouted back, lifting him in the air and spinning him.

The two of them laughed, truly laughing, for the first time in months. At that moment, Thomas felt something stir inside him.

Hope.

16

LATE NIGHT STUDY

It had been a few days since Elias discovered the truth about Decay. The revelation ignited a fire in him, a drive to uncover what was happening to Thomas. The fact that something existed outside his understanding was all the motivation he needed. For nights on end, the two had been poring over ancient texts, barely sleeping. Elias had identified the aura as void magic, an illegal, pitch-black energy that erased things from existence. But the question remained: What was being removed from Thomas's life?

Thomas sat silently, eyes scanning lines of fading ink, sleep tugging at him like waves against a tired swimmer. The Sandman was winning. Days and nights blurred together, fatigue settled deep into his bones. Across the table, Elias nursed black coffee from a to-go mug, leafing through old tomes from the school's restricted archives. Spotting Thomas dozing off, he slid the coffee toward him and nodded.

Thomas's eyes flicked between the mug and Elias. After a beat of contemplation and desperation, he took a tentative sip.

The bitterness made him wince, his mouth opening to release a puff of steam.

"Exactly what I expected," Thomas muttered, pushing the mug away and folding his arms.

Elias rolled his eyes and returned to his reading. "You know, this book claims magic originates from something deeper."

Thomas, propped up by his palm, barely feigned interest. "Like what?"

"Gods. Ancient beasts. The Vikings had multiple theories. None were ever confirmed."

"What's that got to do with me?"

"Well, Algernon believed in interbreeding between humans and mages."

That got Thomas's attention. In mage society, such unions were taboo and seen as reckless and dangerous. "Probably just didn't care," he replied, brushing it off.

"Maybe. But Algernon was the only mage community that supported it."

Before Elias could elaborate, a loud *thud* interrupted them. A book dropped heavily on a nearby table, making them both jump. Brody stood there.

"Sup, sup. Looks like you two are on a study binge too."

Thomas noticed something off. Brody wasn't his usual self. He didn't meet their eyes the same way. He looked...tense.

"Yeah, just brushing up on mage history," Thomas lied, guarding the truth. As much as he loved his friends, being vulnerable with them felt too close to how it felt back at the orphanage, like being pitied. They'd always loved him, sure, but they'd also stopped believing he'd ever be adopted. Now, it was the same story in a different setting. This time, it was about his aura.

Brody nodded, voice a little too casual. "Cool. Mind if I join you?"

He wasn't just bored. Deep down, Brody felt inadequate. Overshadowed by his friends, by their power, by his family's expectations. He needed to grow stronger to prove he wasn't a mistake.

"Sure," Elias said finally, breaking the awkward silence. "I'm gonna grab more coffee."

Once Elias left, the library settled into its usual quiet, the hum of students coming and going in the distance. The library itself was a cathedral of knowledge, fiction, nonfiction, and the arcane, spanning generations of mage history.

Brody flipped through a book on the nature of magical auras. It was nothing new to him: hybrid magic, aura transmission, and how mages tapped into the world's natural energy. Aura flowed like water through a fountain: released through spells and replenished from nature. But each person's aura storage was different, and while it could be trained, Brody's family believed true potential was genetic.

Time passed unnoticed. Brody glanced up at Thomas, who was now asleep. At first, he was going to wake him until he saw something strange.

Thomas twitched. A translucent aura seeped from his eyes and mouth, colorless, like heat waves. Brody froze. *Does he have an aura, after all?*

The aura wrapped around the book under Thomas's head, pulsing. A wave of unnatural energy rippled across the room. The words on the page liquefied, slipping into Thomas's ears. Brody's thoughts spun. This was impossible. No one could absorb a mage book like that. Not legally. Not magically.

Startled, Brody's knee banged into the table. He grimaced.

The impact broke the trance Thomas stirred, and the aura retreated. The words reformed on the page.

"Sorry," Brody said, rubbing his leg. "Hit my knee."

Before he could decide whether to tell Thomas what he'd seen, Elias returned.

"Let's call it a night. I'll return the books. Let's get back to the dorm," Elias said, seeing Thomas barely conscious.

"I'll do it," Brody offered quickly. "You get him home."

Thomas mumbled in exhaustion as Elias lifted him.

"Thanks," Elias said, smiling.

Brody watched them go, his smile fading. He turned to the book *The Ancient Burials of Mages and* read the back: *An Exploration of Forgotten Cults, Tombs, and Hidden Magical Societies.* Sitting in Thomas's chair, Brody ran his hands over the cover.

I need to tell them what I saw, he told himself. But he didn't move.

Instead, he whispered, "I need to catch up."

The decision snapped into place. "Screw it."

He closed his eyes, and his yellow aura enveloped the book. The words melted from the pages, flowing into his ears.

Suddenly, he was there inside the book's memory. A mysterious island. Raw, untamed aura hummed through the trees, brushing against his skin like silk. Ahead, two men and twins argued, shoving one another.

One drew a dagger black handle, silver blade, and purple runes etched into the steel. *Soul,* Brody read.

The blade sank into one twin's stomach. His body crumpled, soul sucked into the blade. The murderer walked toward a hidden forest cave. Brody followed.

He knew this man or felt like he did. The shredded armor, the claw marks. When he tried to focus on his face, it blurred like a dream.

At the cave's mouth, the man placed his palm on the stone. A glowing imprint appeared.

Brody stepped closer and then snapped back into his body. Gasping, eyes wide, he found the book closed beneath him.

The last page.

His skin tingled. The knowledge was burned into him, not like reading, more like *living* the memory.

Was this normal for aura absorption? Was that figure the book's author?

He leaned back in his chair, staring at the ceiling, heart pounding.

He hadn't found clarity. He'd opened a door.

And now... he wasn't sure it could be closed.

17

FIST FIGHTS, AURA BLASTS

The cafeteria was deathly quiet.

Eva and Mari sat eating their food, Elias sipped his coffee while reading a book, Brody and Silas simply stared at the table in silence, and Thomas sat with his face buried in his hands, utterly exhausted.

The school had entered its final stretch of intense studies of history, and color magic dominated the curriculum. While most of the group was managing decently, Thomas couldn't use magic for the practical parts of the exams, and Brody was failing the knowledge components. The others were holding on, but barely.

It wasn't just the exams weighing them down.

Everyone was tangled up in a deeper mystery: Mari wore the ring she had found, Brody wrestled with the history and the haunting knowledge he absorbed, and Thomas struggled with the runes embedded in his bones. The crew wasn't just losing hope for Thomas; they were starting to lose hope for themselves.

No one looked at each other.

The soft tapping of Thomas's knee against the bottom of the table grew louder and louder, the rapid beat of rising anxiety. Decay, the sinister figure haunting Thomas, was now a constant shadow. Elias managed to ignore the specter, but Thomas couldn't. He kept his eyes fixed downward, terrified of seeing him.

Brody had stopped meeting Thomas's eyes altogether. Guilt and pain gnawed at him; the secret he kept burned in his gut. He felt like a terrible friend, yet he clung to his progress in strength training as some small redemption.

He wasn't even sure if the magic boost had come from the mysterious book he'd absorbed. It felt more like blind survival than growth.

Mari, meanwhile, was swallowed by the mystery of her father. The weight of the unknown pressed heavily on her: what secrets lay behind her father's incident? And what did it mean to be the only half-human, half-mage student at Blackwood? Her thumb rubbed endlessly over the emblem of the ring, her eyes distant and heavy with tension.

James and his goons had been unusually quiet lately.

But that was only because the entire school had shunned Thomas. No one spoke to him. Teachers ignored him. His name disappeared from rosters and attendance lists. It was clear: unless Thomas somehow broke the runes by the end of the year, he wouldn't be returning.

Even Castel had grown quiet, claiming he was trying to arrange a meeting with the principal.

But gaining an audience with the principal of Blackwood, one of only three magical academies in the world, was like petitioning royalty. Principal Magnus Thorne wasn't just a leader; he was a figure of immense knowledge, secrets, and authority.

To Thomas, it felt like trying to reach a President or, worse, a dictator.

And now, no teacher, no staff member, would lift a finger to help him.

Elias rose to grab more coffee, eyes locked on his liquid salvation.

But then a sharp sting wrapped around his head, and before he could react, the floor rushed up to meet him. He slammed into the ground with a sickening crash, the sound ricocheting through the silent cafeteria.

James, Gerald, and Piggy stood behind him. Piggy's fist was still balled, the punch that felled Elias fresh on his knuckles.

The cafeteria stirred with whispers.

"Watch where you're going, nerd!" James shouted.

"You belong at that table with the orphan," Piggy sneered.

Piggy's face had mostly healed since Thomas's earlier confrontation, but the crooked set of his nose remained a permanent reminder.

Elias dazed, clutched the back of his head.

Thomas stood without thinking.

The others flinched, scrambling to rise and stop him, but it was too late. The blind fury in Thomas's eyes was unmistakable.

Piggy turned too slowly.

Thomas's fist crashed into his cheek, sending him sprawling onto the ground.

In the same motion, Thomas's wand flicked in his hand. A surge of brown aura erupted, splintering the floor beneath James and launching him backward onto his back.

"I'm sick of this, James!" Thomas roared, his voice thundering through the cafeteria. "You and me right here, right now!"

"Leave him alone, fake mage!" a voice jeered.

A cafeteria tray spun through the air like a frisbee toward Thomas's head.

But before it could connect, Brody's hand snatched it out of the air with a flick of the wrist, sending it hurtling back into the face of the original thrower.

And then chaos truly erupted.

James scrambled up, throwing jabs.

Thomas tackled him, fists flying as they crashed through trash cans and rolled across the floor.

Brody engaged Piggy, the two slamming into each other with all the brute force of wrestlers.

Some students tried to break up the fights; others eagerly jumped into the fray.

Silas grabbed a dazed Elias and dragged him away from the melee.

Gerald fired off a blast of burning red aura toward Brody and Piggy, but it was smothered mid-air by a gush of water.

Mari stood firm, a blue aura dripping from her fingertips, locking eyes with Gerald. She defended the bystanders and blocked anyone else from joining the fight.

Eva was perched atop two unconscious classmates, smiling brightly as she cheered Thomas on.

The battle was intense, fast, and ugly.

It felt endless, but it lasted only minutes before a deafening sonic boom shook the room.

Thomas, who had been pinning James to the ground, was blasted off him.

Brody and Piggy crashed to the floor in a heap.

Auras flickered and vanished, leaving the cafeteria heavy and silent.

Heavy footsteps echoed across the room.

A massive figure stepped forward:

Salt-and-pepper goatee, piercing silver eyes, short hair, and a sharp suit with a golden pocket watch glinting in his hand.

Principal Magnus Thorne, in the flesh.

His aura washed over the cafeteria like a tidal wave.

Everyone collapsed to their knees under the unbearable weight, breathless, trembling, powerless.

Behind him stood Castel, disappointment etched on his face.

"I think it's time we settle this once and for all," Magnus declared, his voice not angry but commanding.

"One month," he said, pacing slowly before them.

"In one month, we will host a tournament. You'll fight this out in an official duel."

He let the words sink into the stunned silence.

"If Thomas and his friends win he stays. If James or any of his friends win, Thomas will be expelled and sent back to the human world."

The weight of the words crushed the air from Thomas's lungs.

How had it come to this without ever meeting the man? His future was being decided in an instant.

"Deal," James said immediately, a cocky smirk curling across his face.

"Fine," Thomas spat back.

The others nodded slowly.

Principal Thorne remained silent a moment longer, then crouched between Thomas and James, staring deep into their souls.

"From now until the tournament," he said, "you two will

not exchange a single word. The tournament will decide everything."

There was something in his tone not a warning to Thomas but a threat aimed at James.

Then he stood, turned, and walked away.

When he disappeared, the crushing weight lifted, and everyone slowly, shakily, raised their heads.

Castel lingered only a moment longer before leaving as well.

The cafeteria remained in stunned, hollow silence.

Thomas and his friends on one side; James, Gerald, Piggy, and three others on the other.

Quietly, everyone began to clean the wreckage around them.

But the thought was the same in every mind:

Thomas might not be here much longer.

After the mess was cleared, the group stood awkwardly, not meeting each other's eyes.

Thomas turned and left first.

Elias followed quickly behind.

Mari hesitated, tears welling up in her eyes, fists clenched, then stormed off in the opposite direction.

Eva watched after them, fidgeting with her fingers, before choosing to follow Mari.

Brody sat heavily at a table, Silas sliding in beside him.

"Thomas is gonna get kicked out," Brody said finally, his voice flat.

Silas frowned but didn't meet his eyes. "Don't say that," he muttered, trying to sound brave but sounding more scared than anything else.

"We just have to win the tournament," Silas insisted. "And you're one of the str-"

"No, I'm not!" Brody snapped, cutting him off. "I can't stand on the same ground as Thomas or Mari."

He buried his face in his hands.

"Thomas is better with a wand than I'll ever be with aura alone."

Silas fell quiet, guilt clawing at his chest.

"Sorry," was all he could whisper.

"Mari!" Eva called, running after her.

"What's wrong?"

Mari froze, forcing Eva to skid to a halt behind her.

"I let my emotions get the best of me," Mari choked out, voice shaking. "I got involved in a stupid fight!"

Eva frowned and rested a hand on Mari's shoulder.

"It wasn't stupid. It was for Elias."

But Mari wasn't listening.

"Thomas is going to get kicked out," she cried. "And Castel… Castel's never going to look at us the same way again!"

Tears streamed down her face as she buried it in her hands.

Eva stood there quietly, holding her tightly.

"Half-mage, full-mage, it doesn't matter," Eva whispered. "You're the strongest and smartest mage I know."

Mari sniffed, gulping down her tears, and finally began to walk again, Eva close behind.

Thomas marched across the school grounds toward the open field between the forest and the farm.

Elias trailed after him, struggling to keep up.

"Where are we going?" Elias asked.

Thomas didn't answer.

His breathing was heavy; his eyes were locked on the trees ahead.

His wand slid from his pocket into his hand.

"I'm not going home!" Thomas shouted.

He reached the center of the field, thrust his wand forward, and unleashed a blast of aura at the trees, which were flashing wildly: red sparks, water droplets, and crackling lightning.

"I'm not going home, Elias!" he yelled again, the blast shifting colors violently.

Another surge of aura ripped from his wand, heat and vibration tearing through his bones.

He was nearing his limit.

Thomas could feel it

The breaking point was coming.

18

CHEATERS EVERYWHERE

"Did you hear Thomas caused a riot in the cafeteria?"

"I heard he was using aura!"

"No, I heard he was using illegal magic!"

"And the rest of his friends? They're helping him hide it!"

The rumors were spreading like wildfire in the dry season. The entire school was buzzing. Whispers swirled about how the principal had to intervene, and word of the tournament swept through the halls. The atmosphere grew hostile, not just for Thomas but for everyone close to him. For the first time since school began, the others were starting to feel the isolation Thomas had known all along.

The library was packed with students preparing for finals. But Mari wasn't studying equations or magical history. She was buried in books on cults, secret societies, factions, and ancient symbols. She was trying to match the emblem on her ring to anything in recorded history. Her fingers flipped pages rapidly, scanning for images or phrases that stood out. She wasn't reading so much as combing through layers of forgotten lore.

Book after book blurred by until a hand touched her shoulder. Mari jolted up, fists clenched, ready to strike, until she saw Eva, who quickly threw her arms up like a trained fighter.

Mari sighed and lowered her fists. She dropped back into her seat. "What are you doing here? Are you okay?"

Eva sat beside her, glancing over the scattered books with a frown. "You've been acting weird lately," she said, gently taking Mari's hand. "Is this about Thomas and the tournament?"

"It's not," Mari snapped. Eva recoiled, her hands retreating into her lap. Guilt flickered across Mari's face. She exhaled. "I'm sorry. I just... have a lot on my mind."

She slipped the ring off her finger and placed it on the table. Eva's gaze dropped to it.

"I've been meaning to ask," she said cautiously. "What does that emblem mean? I've seen it a few times."

Mari reacted instantly. "Where? Where have you seen it?" Her eyes were wide, almost frantic.

Eva blinked, startled. She glanced around nervously. "It was in an old book Castel left behind in the cafeteria... a few months ago."

Mari leaned forward, consumed by the possibility.

"And," Eva continued hesitantly, "if you look at the stones near the summoning platform... it's imprinted in the cement."

Mari dropped back into her seat. Her pulse thundered. Could the emblem be tied to the school's founders?

She stared at the table, her hands frozen. Then she looked back at Eva's concerned face. It was time to stop keeping secrets.

"Let me start from the beginning," she said softly.

Mari told Eva everything from her father's execution by Mage authorities to her research into the Algernons and their theories about hybrid bloodlines producing stronger magic. She poured out everything, her words spilling like water from a broken dam.

By the time she was done, Eva was holding her hand again.

"After finals and the tournament," she said with quiet determination, "we're going to have a busy summer."

Brody stood at the forest gates, eyes locked on the tree line. A week ago, while researching for a school project, he found an old photo of a handprint burned into the stone of a temple deep in the woods.

Since then, he'd come out here every day, staring toward the forbidden forest. He needed to know what was out there.

Beside him, Silas fidgeted. "Brody, what's the big deal about this handprint? I mean, really?"

Brody didn't look at him. "It's not that it's important. I just think... something's out there."

The forest was off-limits to first-years, but that didn't stop him from wandering.

A figure emerged from the trees. Brody's hand shot out, grabbing Silas's arm. Castel stepped into view, casual as ever, flicking a lazy wave with fingers emerging from the pocket of his black jeans.

"Hey guys," he said.

Brody wasted no time. "Castel. What's out there?"

Castel raised a brow. He stepped through the gate and shut it behind him. With a flick of his aura-infused finger, now shaped like a key, he locked it.

"It's a sanctuary for magical wildlife," he said. "Most are endangered or extinct in the human world."

Brody folded his arms. "No. I'm talking about the temple."

Castel's smile faded. "That's for next year's lesson. Why are you so interested now?"

"I need to see the warrior's handprint," Brody said, stepping closer.

Castel looked down, his hair falling in front of his face. Then he smiled faintly. "Brody... I can't let you in. Not without a teacher's permission."

As Castel walked past, he patted Brody's shoulder.

"Damn," Brody muttered.

Silas stepped forward. Quietly, his finger shifted into a key. He unlocked the gate.

Brody's jaw dropped. "How did you do?"

"I... cloned his aura," Silas said, cheeks flushed.

Cloning aura required perfect memory and precision. It was rare for prodigies to be born.

Brody stared at him, stunned. "That makes you a genius."

Silas looked down, embarrassed. "Yes..."

They followed the narrow path through the woods. Silas was mesmerized by the magical creatures. A dodo strutted by and breathed fire in Brody's direction. The flames splashed harmlessly against a magical barrier lining the path.

After a mile, they reached a moss-covered temple built over a cave. Brody traced the weathered pillars, eyes wide. Engravings of broken clocks and hourglasses littered the stone.

And there it was: the burned handprint. Preserved in the center of the structure, the temple was built around it like a shrine.

"Should I touch it?" Brody asked.

"No. Why would you touch it?"

"Maybe it has power."

"Brody, it's just a handprint."

"You're just a handprint."

"What are you, five?"

"What are you, five?"

Silas groaned, face in his hands.

Brody crossed his arms. "I thought this would be like a cutscene in a game. Some kind of magic revelation."

"You're already strong in your own way," Silas offered.

Brody rolled his eyes. Still, he appreciated the sentiment.

"Let's grab food," Silas said. "Then we'll study for exams together."

Brody nodded. "Yeah... maybe you're right."

Aura blasted across the training field, changing color and form mid-air. On one end stood Thomas, wand ready. On the other, Elias matched his moves. They were practicing aura-switching, a dangerous technique. Pick the wrong aura at the wrong moment, and you'd get blasted.

Thomas found that out the hard way. He launched a red-hot strike, only for Elias to switch to blue thick and fluid and absorb the blast. Thomas flew back, landing hard.

"That's five for me, three for you," Elias called out.

Thomas coughed, wet and winded. "Last week I couldn't even score one, so I'll take it."

Elias grinned. "We're getting close to finals and the tournament. How do you feel?"

Thomas pointed his wand at himself, using a red aura to dry his clothes. "Confidence. I think I've got a shot at coming back next year."

Elias smiled. Then he froze.

Goosebumps raced up his spine.

"Someone broke the ward on our room," he said.

Without another word, they took off running.

"Open a portal!" Thomas shouted.

Elias thrust his hand forward. A glowing orange portal burst open.

They jumped through and landed outside their dormitory. The door was cracked open.

"No one should be able to bypass the ward," Elias said, tense. "Unless... they're powerful."

Thomas readied his wand. Elias clenched his aura-wrapped fists.

They burst in, ready to fight, but the room was empty.

Then they saw it: a gold pocket watch on Thomas's pillow.

Elias locked the door behind them.

Thomas picked it up, eyes narrowing.

"Open it," Elias said quietly.

Inside was a folded textbook page titled "Suppression Magic." It described how ancient royals suppressed magic in heirs until certain conditions awakened it. Alongside it was a bone fragment with a rune.

Thomas recoiled as pain seared through his body. He dropped the pocketwatch and the bone laying in it.

Elias snatched it up and examined it. At 10:49, the watch's hands were frozen. The engraved "E" on the case twisted the pit in Thomas's stomach.

"That's the watch from my dream," he whispered. "When you were... dead."

The room was thick with dread.

Someone had broken into their sanctuary. Someone knew. Someone was watching.

They sat in silence, staring at each other. A week remained before the tournament.

And nothing made sense anymore.

19

THE FIRST FIGHT

There was a fresh scent in the air on the morning of the tournament. Students hadn't stopped talking about it since the principal's announcement, and the early start only confirmed how serious it was. Spring dew settled on the grass, birds chirped high above, and in the distance near the academy's sports arena, mages worked to convert the field. Painted lines were drawn, wards erected, and food stalls assembled in preparation for the arriving crowd.

Tournaments were common in the mage world. They were ritualistic, regulated, and rooted in the Viking tradition of holmgang, a method of settling disputes through duels. With tensions between James and Thomas finally reaching a breaking point, this was the only path left.

Thomas had barely slept the night before. None of them had. The anxiety was too sharp, the stakes too high to leave anything to chance. It had to go right for him.

He was the first to reach the arena that morning, the golden sun warming his back as he sat in the stands, trying to steady his nerves. His thumb absently stroked the cover of his pocket watch while his mind wandered. So many questions. So few answers.

He stood up, descending the concrete stairs toward the locker rooms. The matchups would be posted soon, the first fight scheduled for 9 a.m. Each step thudded beneath his feet, slow and deliberate, like his body already knew the weight of what was to come.

The underground corridor was cold and utilitarian, built of heavy stone and cement used for storage, events, and sports gatherings. He passed a few students prepping for the big day before stopping in front of a bulletin board plastered with the fight schedule.

Matchups:
Elias vs. Gerald
Brody vs. Preston ("Piggy")
Marco vs Henry (Two kids apart of the cafeteria fight)
Winner of Elias/Gerald vs. winner of the cafeteria match
Mari vs. Alice (another cafeteria brawl participant)
Thomas vs. Lance (also from the cafeteria fight)
James vs. Brody or Preston
Final: Thomas vs. winner of the cafeteria bracket

Seven battles. Ten possible opponents before Thomas even stepped onto the field. It was going to be a battle for the ages, and he would have to watch it unfold first. By the time he fought, he might be facing James and his entire clique.

His stomach twisted. Nausea crept in as anxiety pressed against his ribs. He clutched his midsection. Then, a hand landed on his shoulder, Elias.

The look on Elias's face said everything. No matter what happened, he wasn't going down without a fight.

"Glad to see you're awake," Thomas said with a faint smile.

"Yeah, well, had to rest a little longer because of your snoring," Elias teased, scanning the board.

"Looks like a pretty decent bracket."

Thomas nodded, following Elias into the locker room. One by one, the rest of the group trickled in. Thankfully, the teams were separated, Thomas's crew in one locker room, James's in the other.

Brody arrived next. He wasn't his usual enthusiastic self, something that had been fading for a while now. Then came Mari, looking slightly dissociated. Silas and Eva had opted out of the tournament entirely, unwilling to deal with the pressure. Thomas understood, but it made their side feel weaker.

The room was tense, and the ticking wall clock only amplified the stillness. Above them, the crowd grew louder, their excitement shaking the stands.

At 8:50, a teacher pushed open the locker room door and looked straight at Elias.

"Let's go."

Elias nodded and followed them out, ascending the stone steps that led to the battlefield.

Thomas's heart dropped. Elias was up first, and his performance would be a sign. If he and Brody could win, maybe Thomas stood a chance at staying. He picked up a remote and turned on the locker room TV, which broadcasted the arena live. The stadium was packed. The sun beamed brightly across the field. Thomas's hopes faltered anyway.

"Alright everyone!" bellowed Magnus Vale, the battle-worn instructor, clapping her hands with a thunderous burst of aura.

The magical barrier surrounding the stands shimmered in response.

She wore a headset mic; her voice echoed powerfully across the stadium. "This tournament will settle a long-standing feud between two classmates!" she announced. "Like our Viking ancestors, we settle disputes through combat. This is not a duel to the death. The first to yield or fall unconscious loses!"

The rules were simple: fight, fall, or forfeit. But magic made every blow potentially lethal.

"First match Elias versus Gerald!"

Cheers erupted. Stomping feet pounded like war drums across the island.

The metal gates creaked open. Elias stepped out with his hands in his pockets. On the other end, Gerald mirrored him as calm, quiet, and controlled.

"Fight!" Magnus shouted.

A shockwave of aura burst between the fighters. Gerald struck first a beam of brilliant red fire magic, the purest and fastest form. It sizzled across the field, embers trailing.

Elias clapped his hands together. A burst of dark blue aura compressed water met Gerald's attack. The beam split in two. He countered with a slicing wave of liquid, his aura dripping from his fingertips like enchanted sludge.

Gerald crossed his arms. A golden-brown aura formed gauntlets on his forearms, metal magic, and armor conjuration. Elias's slice slammed into them, denting but not breaking.

The duel was fierce, and neither wanted to get close. Long-range attacks flew back and forth. Bursts of aura lit the air, and the barrier flickered as it absorbed the impact.

Then contact was made. Elias crashed into the barrier, blood pouring from a deep gash in his right arm. His fingers tingled;

his arm went numb.

Gerald hesitated, ready to strike, but stopped. He wasn't cruel.

"The winner is Gerald!" Magnus roared.

The crowd erupted again. Elias blinked back tears.

Two mages rushed to his side, healing magic glowing green as they sealed the wound. Elias winced but sighed in relief. As he was helped off the field, Thomas stared at the screen. So did the others.

If Elias, the most gifted aura user among them, couldn't win... what chance did the rest have?

"Knowing something and demonstrating it aren't the same as surviving a real fight," Brody muttered, breaking the silence. "But we can still pull this off."

He meant to encourage them, but no one quite believed it.

Thomas clutched his stomach, eyes fixed on the locker room doors. Elias's match had lasted five minutes. And in five minutes, the first line of defense had fallen. In an hour, Thomas might be packing his bags for the orphanage.

The door opened. A teacher locked eyes with Brody.

"Let's go."

Brody stood, nodding to the others. He took a deep breath and walked through the doors. He was nervous more than anyone knew. But buried under the nerves was something else.

A quiet voice in the back of his head whispered that it didn't really matter to him whether Thomas stayed or not.

At the steel gates, he stared out at the field.

"Next up: Brody versus Preston!"

The crowd roared.

'Preston?' Brody thought. He'd never known Piggy's real name.

The gates opened slowly.

'Now or never,' Brody told himself.

20

PIGGLY WIGGLY

Brody stepped out through the gates, walking onto the battle-field. Across from him, Piggy slammed his fists together, rolled his shoulders, and cracked his neck with a vicious grin. With his crooked nose courtesy of Thomas and yellow-stained teeth, he looked like someone hungry for vengeance. He marched to his side of the arena, radiating menace. Off to the side, Magnus Vale rubbed her hands together eagerly.

"Alright, everyone FIGHT!" she screamed, her voice echoing through the stadium.

To say things escalated faster than expected was an un-derstatement. Piggy's body flared with a yellow aura, static crackling around him as his hair stood on end. In a flash, he rocketed forward like a bullet fired from a gun.

Brody took a deep breath and raised his arms. A soft, pastel-pink aura surged through him, his blood pumping faster, strength gathering in his forearms. Piggy's fist slammed into him, sending shockwaves rippling outward and denting the ground beneath their feet.

The crowd erupted. With cheers and screams, it was clear this was going to be brutal. Brody responded by flaring his aura outward, forcing Piggy's arms wide and exposing his center. Brody's fist connected with Piggy's chest, but something was off. The impact didn't land as hard as expected.

Piggy concentrated his aura at the point of contact. His body began to glow a hot pink, his eyes bloodshot, and his face flushed red.

"Berserk!" Piggy roared.

The real battle had just begun.

Berserk is a dangerous state where the user's energy rapidly drains in exchange for greater strength, heightened aggression, and a total loss of pain perception.

Blow after blow rained down on Brody: fists to his stomach, to his arms, relentless. He couldn't land a counter, but he managed to keep his green aura flowing, using it to heal himself in real-time. He'd have to outlast Piggy. That was the only way.

"This is hard to watch," Thomas said quietly to Mari.

She nodded, wincing with each blow Brody endured. "He's holding his own, though. Using healing magic to regenerate is smart even for Brody."

Thomas didn't respond. He watched in silence, eyes locked on the arena. Brody was struggling. Everyone could see it.

"Maybe I should just forfeit and end this," he muttered, burying his face in his hands.

Mari turned to him, disbelief on her face. "What are you saying?"

Before he could reply, she cut him off. "End it? After everything we've been through?" Her voice rose, sharpened by frustration. "I get it. This Year has been hell for all of us. But Elias and Brody are giving everything, so you have a shot at staying. You're really thinking of giving up now?"

Thomas said nothing. He looked away, sighing deeply. She was right, and he knew it. Despite all the tension and the fractured trust, they were still fighting for him.

Brody crashed to the ground and rolled, springing back to his feet. He grabbed Piggy's wrists, but a brutal kick to his gut sent him flying again.

His brain was struggling to keep up. Every second, every strike, Piggy was faster and stronger. Brody swung, kicked, and pivoted, but nothing landed. Everything was getting countered.

Then came the blow to the face. Blood spattered against the barrier. Brody's ears rang. Piggy was laughing, saying something but Brody couldn't hear it. His vision swam.

I need to be stronger.

But that wasn't the answer. Strength wouldn't win this. Not today.

Am I faster?

Electricity crackled around him. Yellow aura wrapped his body.

He took off, sprinting around the stadium. The crowd roared again.

BAM!

His fist crashed into Piggy's ribs, and he didn't stop moving. The crowd gasped. Piggy stumbled.

Brody zipped back and forth, striking: ribs, face, knees, any exposed point. Piggy's frustration mounted with each hit.

But Brody's speed had a limit.

A fist caught him in the gut.

The combination of Piggy's power and Brody's momentum felt like something ruptured inside.

Brody's legs gave out. His aura shattered into sparks, his body skidding across the dirt until it slammed against the magical barrier.

Flat on his back, he stared up at the sky.

He could feel his father's gaze burning into him from somewhere in the stands. He was not here to cheer him on but to watch him fail.

Brody knew that much.

His eyes rolled back. The world went black.

"Another loss," Eva muttered from the stands, frowning. "I knew I should've participated."

Elias sat beside her, having arrived just before the match began. "Then why didn't you?"

"Mari told me not to."

The words landed like a stone in Elias's chest. Betrayal. They needed every advantage and Mari had said no.

He said nothing. His gaze returned to the field.

"Mari's up next," Silas said softly. He sat beside Eva, nervously fidgeting. "Do you think she'll win? If not, then..." His voice trailed off, his doubt about Thomas clear.

Elias didn't let it show.

"Don't worry," he said. "Mari and Thomas will win their fights."

Eva nodded. "Yeah. No way they'll lose."

Back in the locker room, Mari stood when her name was called. She walked the empty corridor toward the arena stairs. Ten minutes Brody had lasted ten minutes, and now he was unconscious.

Thomas sat in stunned silence, saying nothing.

Mari could feel the weight of his hope shifting to her. She didn't like it, but she didn't have a choice.

She wouldn't lose.

As she moved through the hallway, a strange stillness fell. The air thickened. The space emptied until only a cloaked figure stood at the stairwell.

Mari slowed.

As she passed, the figure spoke.

"The Broken Hourglass is watching."

She froze.

A white, faceless mask. A dark cloak.

"You possess an heirloom. Prove yourself worthy of the ring."

Mari stared. Questions bubbled to the surface, but she couldn't afford distraction.

Not now.

"When I win this," she said coldly, "I want answers."

She turned, walking up the stairs.

Don't get distracted, Mari.

Just win.

21

MUSIC FOR THE SOUL

The gates creaked open with a rusty groan, the clinking of metal echoing across the arena and amplifying the tension already coiled in Mari's chest. Her opponent, Alice, was a music-user. Taking a long, steadying breath, Mari slapped her cheeks lightly in an attempt to stay sharp. As she stepped into the arena, she spotted Alice approaching from the opposite side, violin and bow in hand. Her long, midnight-black hair swayed with her movements, and her icy blue eyes glinted from across the battlefield.

Mari's ears rang. She wasn't listening to Magnus's voice anymore; she already knew what came next. Her thumb rubbed over the surface of the ring on her finger, her gaze locked on the violin. Alice could wield her magic without it, but with it, she was devastating. Mari's fingers twitched in anticipation.

Then came the call.

"Fight!"

Mari's body dropped through an orange portal that opened beneath her feet. In an instant, she was gone. Across the arena,

Alice raised her violin and played a sharp, deliberate note. A wave of aura bloomed around her like a shield, flickering and alive. Her eyes darted frantically. Mari had vanished.

The crowd roared.

"Where did you go?!" Alice shouted, spinning in place, violin clenched tightly, scanning the field in every direction.

She never thought to look up.

High above the arena, Mari emerged from the clouds, free-falling. Her portal shimmered in the sky like a second sun. As Alice's eyes finally lifted, they widened in disbelief. The violin's bow slid across the strings, releasing a hiss so sharp it cut the air. Aura twisted into the shape of massive, snake-like heads and launched toward Mari.

Mari's body glowed a soft grey. Wind spiraled around her as she manipulated her trajectory using grey magic. She darted and swerved mid-air, narrowly avoiding the monstrous snakes. Her arm stretched forward as if preparing to land directly on Alice.

But that wasn't the plan.

A second orange portal burst open beside Alice. A gust of chilled air blew across the battlefield as Mari shot out of the portal at full speed, reaching for the violin. Her hands closed around its neck, yanking it out of Alice's grip as she slid across the ground, landing hard on her knees. The friction tore through her jeans, scraping skin and drawing blood.

Mari stood, breathing heavily, clutching the violin like a weapon. Her head tilted slightly as she raised it.

"Forfeit," she said coldly, "or I break it."

Alice froze. Her hand lifted slightly as if to summon more magic, then slowly dropped. Her defiant expression crumbled into defeat.

"I forfeit," she whispered, lowering her bow.

The crowd exploded. Cheers thundered through the arena. Mari had won flawlessly.

As the noise swelled, Mari turned her head toward the VIP box, the one tied to the ring she wore. Though its windows were blackened, she could feel the weight of unseen eyes watching her. Slowly, she set the violin down, gaze still fixed on the box, and walked off the field without looking away until she stepped through the gates.

In the stands, Eva and Elias were screaming themselves hoarse.

"She's a natural with an aura!" Eva shouted. "And with everything else she knows it's insane!"

"She should've been way more injured after that fall," she added, flagging down a hot dog vendor.

Elias took over with a casual shrug. "She was using grey magic, which lets you fly, but it's more about wind control. She used it to dodge the aura snakes and slow herself down mid-fall."

Eva paid for her food, nodding while chewing. "Makes sense."

"I'm gonna take Thomas some food before his match starts," she added, slipping away through the crowd.

In the locker room, Thomas paced in slow circles, his chest tight, breath shallow. He tipped his head back, trying to calm the nerves writhing in his stomach. The door creaked open.

Eva peeked in, holding a hot dog with condiments on the side. "Hey..." she said gently, not stepping too far in.

Thomas turned, offering a faint smile. "Hey, Eva. You okay?"

"I'm fine. Just... thought you might want something to eat."

"I... yeah. Yeah, sure. I'll eat." He didn't want to seem ungrateful, and besides, he hadn't realized how hungry he was.

He took a bite, then another, almost inhaling it. She handed him a bottle of water, and he drank between mouthfuls. The food steadied him a little.

"Thanks, Eva," he muttered. "Everything's riding on Mari now."

"I wouldn't say that," she replied softly. "You can do this."

He nodded. He didn't believe her, not really, but he didn't want to disappoint her either. Resting a hand on her arm, he gave a quiet nod. "You're right. I can do this."

"I should get going," she said, pausing at the door. "But remember, this tournament isn't over until you and James face off."

James was still a few matches away, but the thought made Thomas smile faintly. "Yeah. James is gonna lose his teeth."

She grinned and slipped out. When the door clicked shut, the tension returned like a wave. Thomas clenched his fists. Truthfully, he had little faith in himself.

Elsewhere, in the medical bay, Brody jolted awake, chest heaving, heart hammering. The vision from the book still clung to his thoughts like smoke. Blinking, he looked toward the television screen mounted on the wall that was playing a replay of Mari's duel.

She made it look easy.

He sat up slowly, swinging his legs over the side of the bed. Shame settled over him like a blanket.

He had tried so hard to prove himself. But even at his best, it wasn't enough.

He stood, each step heavy, and walked out of the medical ward. The roar of the crowd grew faint behind him as he left the stadium, burdened by guilt, disappointment, and the hollow ache of failure.

CHAPTER 22

22

Accidental Sabotage

Thomas could feel his nerves spiking. With his battle coming up, the tension was almost unbearable. As he stepped out of the locker room and made his way through the halls of the underground arena, everything around him felt like a blur. His heart pounded in his ears. He had no real way of knowing if he'd win at this point; everything felt like it was riding on Mari's shoulders.

Lost in thought, he didn't notice Castel until he bumped into him. The group hadn't seen Castel in a while. No one really knew why, though they assumed he was upset over the cafeteria brawl that had sparked the whole tournament. Thomas looked up at him, then quickly looked away in shame.

Castel met his eyes and frowned. He placed a hand gently on Thomas's shoulder and gave a small smile. "Hey, Thomas. Cheer up."

Thomas gave a weak frown. "You're not upset?"

Castel shook his head. "I came down here to find you and Mari, actually. To give you both a little motivation."

There was a pause. Thomas struggled to stay present. His

anxiety was too loud, too heavy to tune out.

"I'm sorry about the fight," he finally said, glancing toward the arena entrance.

"Don't be," Castel replied. "None of that matters anymore. What matters is that you're going in there and you're going to win this."

Castel spoke with a confidence that Thomas didn't feel in himself. Thomas stood still for a moment, then nodded. "Yeah... okay."

But his voice betrayed him. Castel could hear how off he sounded. He looked pale and unsteady like he was on the edge of shutting down completely.

Without a word, Castel pulled him into a hug. Thomas didn't have time to react, his body moved on its own. His face pressed into Castel's shoulder, and the tears came instantly. Hot and fast, they soaked through Castel's shirt. Thomas sobbed, gasping for breath like a small child who couldn't stop crying. His grip tightened around Castel's back.

"You have nothing to prove," Castel whispered. "You don't need to prove anything to anyone. Win or lose, it doesn't matter. I'll visit you every summer from here on out, okay? I'll teach you myself if I have to."

The words hit Thomas like a defibrillator to the chest. Thomas felt something shift. His body trembled, and the sound of his heartbeat finally slowed. The world's weight seemed just a bit lighter.

He took a deep breath and stepped back, wiping his eyes. Castel placed a firm hand on his shoulder.

"I believe in you. So go win."

Thomas's eyes widened. Something stirred inside him, something fierce and unfamiliar. Confidence.

Elias. Eva. Mari. Brody. Silas. They all believed in him. But Castel's belief felt different. It reached deeper.

Thomas nodded. "I will."

With renewed focus, he walked toward the steps, his head held high, and his hand clenched tightly around his wand.

The crowd noise grew louder with every step. The cold steel gate loomed ahead. The battlefield had been reset. He could hear Magnus speaking but didn't pay attention. His ears were tuned to the chants. They were calling Lance's name.

The gate opened. Thomas stepped into the sunlight. Across the field, Lance stood scrawny, with a buzz cut, hoodie, and jeans. Their eyes met.

"Fight!" Magnus's voice rang out.

Lance sprinted toward him, pink aura flaring with heavy-striking intent. Thomas stood still. He had trained with Elias. The wand was meant to help children channel aura, not serve as a crutch. But Thomas had learned something: wands had no real limitations. If you trained hard enough, you could do anything with one.

Lance was only feet away. His fist drew back.

Dust exploded around them.

For a moment, the audience couldn't see anything.

Then the dust cleared.

A black aura radiated from the tip of Thomas's wand, encased in a glowing layer of brown. The crowd gasped. Silence fell.

Thomas stood tall, his wand pointed directly at Lance. He had done it using a hybrid aura through the wand.

"That's what we practiced!" Elias shouted from the stands, triggering a wave of cheers and boos.

From the ground, black void metal shot up and wrapped around Lance's wrists, ankles, and throat, locking him in place.

Thomas didn't let up. The aura streamed steadily from his wand, his bones vibrating violently under the pressure.

"How? Wands aren't supposed to sync with hybrid magic!" Silas exclaimed.

Eva, on the other hand, was too busy screaming. "Punch him in the jaw, Thomas!" she yelled, violently shaking the poor student in front of her.

Elias watched, shaking his head at her antics before focusing back on the match. "I can't explain it. It's like something inside him adjusts the wand's frequencies to stabilize the aura. But it won't last long. Hybrid magic will eventually shatter the wand."

Thomas stepped closer to Lance, the restraints holding him firm. He placed a hand on his face and looked around.

"I think I will win," he said clearly.

There was hesitation. The teachers didn't immediately call it.

Then, finally, Magnus lifted her headset. "Thomas is the WINNER!"

The arena erupted with cheers, boos, and shouts. Some were inspired. Others were furious. Accusations of cheating were already being muttered.

Still, Thomas had won.

He released the aura, and Lance collapsed, breathing heavily. As Thomas turned to leave, he heard Lance's voice behind him.

"Hey."

Thomas looked over his shoulder. "Yeah?"

"Did you really use that wand for that?"

"Yeah. Why?"

Lance's face twisted with anger, but Thomas turned and kept walking. The crowd noise changed; it was no longer cheers. It was shouts, screams, and warnings.

He spun just in time to see the flash of yellow.

A bolt of lightning aura fired at him.

Fifteen feet. That's all the distance between them.

He smelled the smoke. Felt the hair on his arms rise. Muscles locked.

The blast hit him square in the chest.

His eyes rolled back.

He hit the dirt face first, the smell of burning wood in his nose.

23

MARI VS GERALD

Thomas was rushed to the infirmary. Thankfully, his injuries weren't life-threatening and could be healed. The stadium erupted in chaos, students shouting, some crying out in disbelief. Eva and Elias bolted down the bleachers, pushing past the crowd to find their friend. On the other side of the field, Lance was immediately restrained by teachers and dragged back toward his section of the arena. No one knew what would happen next. Would the matches continue? The uncertainty left the entire stadium buzzing with restless energy as the faculty gathered at the center of the field to deliberate.

Beneath the arena, in the infirmary, Mari burst through the doors, her eyes locking onto Thomas lying unconscious on a cot. Moments later, Brody followed, panting as he stepped inside.

"Brody! Where have you been?" she asked, her voice on edge.

"I've been watching... alone," he answered between breaths. His vague explanation was barely processed before Elias and Eva stormed in, startling them both.

"Is he okay?" Elias shouted. Eva glanced from Mari to Brody, searching their faces for answers; none of them had one.

"He'll be fine," said a calm voice from across the room. They all turned to see a woman they hadn't noticed sitting nearby. "Name's Elinor. I'm the school nurse. Your friend will recover. However…" She held up what remained of Thomas's wand.

Elias stepped forward to take it. The wand was shattered, its core destroyed, reduced to cracked wood and fragments.

"It looks like the attacker aimed for the wand, not Thomas. That's what saved him," Elinor said, her expression grim. "Still, he got lucky."

"He sabotaged him on purpose," Elias muttered in disbelief.

"Mari's our only shot now," Eva added, her voice tinged with hopelessness.

"Don't count me out," came a groggy voice from the bed. Thomas sat up slowly, clutching his arm.

"I'll figure something out."

The group turned to him as Elinor rushed forward, trying to ease him back down.

"You need to rest!" she scolded. "That blast could've killed you!"

Thomas reached into his pocket and pulled out a scorched metal pocket watch, its surface blackened with burn marks.

"This took most of the hit," he said.

"Still, you're pushing yourself too hard," Elinor said, clearly annoyed.

"The battle will continue!" a voice rang out from the TV mounted in the corner. "Next up: Mari versus Gerald!"

The announcement cut off any argument about whether the pocket watch had actually saved him. Elinor waved her arms toward the door.

"Out. Now. All of you. Let Thomas rest."

Brody and Elias continued their debate on their way out while Mari quietly turned in the opposite direction, heading for the arena. Her stride was steady, and she was confident. This win would take her to the finals, and she was certain it was already hers.

At the arena gates, she cracked her knuckles and smirked. The gates rumbled as they rose, stone grinding against metal. Mari stepped onto the battlefield just as Gerald did the same from the opposite side.

On the sidelines, Magnus wiped her hands on a cloth and raised her voice. "Fight!"

Mari barely had time to react before she felt a sharp sting across her left arm. Blood trickled between her fingers. 'But the match just started,' she thought, stunned. She glanced down to find a jagged spear of earth embedded in her shoulder.

Gerald stood calmly, hands in his pockets, golden eyes locked on her. A sluggish, brownish aura rippled around him, heavy and untamed, like a beast pacing the ground.

He had struck first, fast and hard.

Mari ripped the spear from her shoulder and tossed it aside. Clutching her arm, she summoned a glowing orange portal beneath her feet, but Gerald was already on her, spinning into a brutal kick under her chin. Her head snapped back, and she hit the ground, tumbling across the field.

'Damn it, Mari,' she scolded herself. She had gotten cocky, and this was the price.

She pushed herself up with her good arm, but her left arm hung limp. Before she could regain her footing, the ground flipped beneath her, launching her into the air. She slammed hard into the arena wall, her sweater tearing as her back struck the dirt.

He was keeping his distance, just like in the cafeteria fight. His aura moved low to the ground, fast and unpredictable.

Mari's gaze drifted toward the VIP box she had broken into weeks ago. "They're watching," she whispered. She recalled the strange man in the hallway. She couldn't lose. Not now.

With a growl, she tore off her ruined sweater, revealing the tank top she wore underneath. Blood dripped freely from her shoulder. She vanished into another portal.

Gerald spun around, his aura forming a wide barrier around him. The crowd murmured in confusion.

"Did she run away?"

"Where'd she go?" Eva asked.

"Look closely at the portal," Elias said. Eva narrowed her eyes and saw two thin portals layered on top of each other.

"She's jumping between them," she realized aloud.

"How does that even work?" Silas asked.

Elias shrugged. "No idea. I've never seen aura manipulation like that."

Suddenly, Gerald's aura flinched when there was a breach. A portal opened beneath his feet, and Mari shot up from it like a bullet. Her fist slammed into his jaw, knocking his teeth together. Before he could recover, another portal opened above him. Mari dropped down, fists clasped, and smashed them into his gut. Blood burst from his lips as he crumpled to the ground.

Mari landed beside him, panting. She pressed her foot against his throat.

"Tap out, or I kick your teeth in."

Her voice was dead serious. Gerald raised a trembling hand in surrender.

The crowd exploded, chanting her name. They had once doubted her, but now, they were starting to believe.

As Mari exited the arena, her hand clutched her injured arm. Reaching the infirmary door, she paused. Something felt off. Auras shifted in the empty hallway. Her breath caught in her throat. Whispers crawled into her ears, growing louder and hotter. The ring on her finger tightened painfully.

The infirmary door opened suddenly. She stumbled backward straight into Thomas, who caught her in his arms.

"Easy there. I was just about to head to the gates," he said, steadying her.

"You okay? You must be dizzy from the blood loss."

She didn't respond, just smiled faintly, patting his back as she passed him.

"Don't die," she whispered before collapsing onto the bed.

24

THOMAS

It was easy for the world to doubt Thomas. James had been dominating every match, and Thomas seemed like nothing more than a cog in the machine. He stood quietly at the gates, his eyes fixed ahead, too afraid to look toward James's side of the arena. Somewhere beyond the barrier, his opponent was preparing. Wandless, Thomas had trained for weeks in the fields with Elias every drop of energy poured into this moment.

The gates began to open slowly. The crowd erupted into chaos. To them, this was the main event, the duel of the tournament. A "fake" mage against someone born and bred for this world. Thomas stepped onto the field, his heart thundering in his chest. The roar of the crowd blurred into a deafening beat in his head, drowning everything else out.

His eyes locked on James, who was already mouthing insults across the field. You're dead, fake mage.

"Fake Mage! Fake Mage! Fake Mage!" the crowd chanted, stomping their feet on the bleachers. Was it mockery or support? Thomas couldn't tell. He scanned the sea of students, hoping to see his friends, needing some anchor to keep him steady but their faces were lost in the crowd.

A breeze swept over his face, a small reminder to breathe. Somewhere in the infirmary, Mari was still in the tournament. Maybe they could still win. He turned back to James. The ringing in his ears grew louder.

"Fight!"

The command cut through the noise, sending a jolt through Thomas's body. He froze, unsure of James's next move. But James didn't strike. He grinned mockingly, dragging it out for the crowd. "Come on, use your wand- oh right," he sneered.

"Fight me! Do something!" James shouted. The taunts and laughter from the stands intensified.

Then, Thomas saw Decay standing behind James like a shadow no one else could see. Dante's form shimmered next to him, evaporating in the breeze. Decay placed his hands on James's head, but James didn't react. Thomas' burns flared painfully. Desperate for something to ground himself, Thomas shoved a hand into his pocket and felt it: the bone shard from the pocket watch.

He pulled it out, stared at it, then clenched it in his fist until blood began to trickle down his palm.

James sneered again. "I'll end this quickly. Don't you worry!"

Pathetic. Pathetic. Pathetic! Thomas berated himself. I can't go home. This is all I have. I was nobody. His vision blurred. I am nobody.

James's aura flared red, fire exploding toward him like a tidal wave.

Pathetic! Pathetic! PATHE-

The drums in Thomas's head shifted, no longer just beating

but revving like an engine. He let out a scream.

"I'm not a fake mage! You'll have to kill me before I leave this school!"

The words exploded across the stadium, silencing the crowd for a brief, breathless moment.

"Then let me grant your wish!" James roared, unleashing his full aura. A roaring wave of fire rushed toward Thomas.

Thomas stood still, bracing for impact.

Then, the world went quiet.

When he opened his eyes, the firewall was frozen midair, a breath away from him. Decay stood in front of it, his gaze fixed on Thomas. His body was slowly unraveling into a colorless aura, fading into the air.

Time had stopped.

Around the stadium, golden glimmers of aura sparkled as if the air itself were glitching. Eva was mid-leap into the arena. Silas had her around the waist, fear frozen on his face. Elias clutched his hair, panicked. In the infirmary, Mari was mid-scream at the TV while Elinor wrapped her injured arm. Brody hid in the shadows, peeking through his fingers. Castel, calm and collected, wore a knowing smirk.

Was I not the only one unaffected by the time shift? Thomas turned slowly, absorbing the scene.

The stillness felt like the moment after killing Dante, haunting, yet peaceful. Tears rolled down his cheeks. Aura began to form in his hands.

"Finally," he whispered.

Facing the frozen fire, he buttoned up his flannel shirt, leaving the top few undone and raised his hands out to his sides. The aura surged. When on defense, a strong enough aura can ripple another's aura, Magnus had once said. Let it flow like it's your own blood, Whitmore's voice echoed.

They had rejected him, but their lessons stuck.

His eyes snapped open. His hands clapped together.

Time resumed.

A wave of purple aura exploded from him. The wall of fire split around his body, slamming harmlessly into the barriers. The crowd gasped.

"James killed him!" someone shouted.

But when the smoke cleared, Thomas stood tall, his aura burning brighter than James's red or yellow ever had. The crowd was stunned, silent.

"You lied!" James screamed, furious. "I'll put you in your place!"

Lightning cracked from James's fingertips. Thomas didn't flinch. He pushed off the ground and glided forward, smooth as skating on ice. His aura felt like home.

He soared across the arena, dancing through blasts of lightning, fire, and shards of earth. He flipped onto the magical barrier, skating across it like it was nothing. The crowd gawked in disbelief.

"What?! Can't fight?" James shouted, growing frantic.

But Thomas was dragging this out; he was enjoying it, the power, the freedom, the air against his skin. He closed his eyes and took it all in.

Then, he launched himself off the barrier. For a second, he was flying, arms outstretched, head first toward the ground. He twisted midair, redirected his momentum, and landed hard behind James in a cloud of smoke.

James spun around, firing a blast of lightning. Thomas deflected it effortlessly and stepped forward.

"Thank you, James," he said quietly.

His palm hit James's chest. His aura surged forward, blasting James back across the field into the barrier. James slumped, unconscious.

Silence.

Thomas put his hands in his pockets.

Then, like instinct, he summoned a black and purple aura, layering them to open a shadowy void in front of him. He stepped through it.

The stadium exploded into cheers. "Fake Mage! Fake Mage!" they chanted, but now it sounded like victory.

The rift opened in the locker room.

Thomas stepped out as it closed behind him.

The door burst open.

"Oh my God, man! You did it!" Elias shouted, more excited than anyone had ever seen him.

Eva threw her arms around his neck, a blush spreading across his cheeks. Mari bounced with joy.

"You won! We won the tournament!" she yelled, punching his arm hard enough to make him wince.

Brody wasn't there.

He had left the stadium, walking away with Silas following close behind. Silas didn't say much; he just cared enough not to leave Brody alone. Brody couldn't help but wonder...was he lying the whole time.

Back in the stadium entrance, Castel stood at the doorway, clapping.

Thomas and the others turned to him.

"Looks like you finally figured that aura out," Castel smirked.

"Guess so. Might grab some blackened chicken strips to replenish it," Thomas shot back with a grin.

Castel ruffled his hair. Just a year older than them, he was still one of the most powerful mages on the island.

"So," Castel said, "You're ending the tournament here, or are you gonna fight Mari for gold?"

Thomas and Mari exchanged a look. A silent beat passed before Thomas offered a hand.

"May the best mage win?"

Mari grinned wide and slapped her hand into his. "As an apology for ever doubting you, I'll take you up on that."

They both smiled, ready for one last duel.

25

MARI VS THOMAS

The crowd roared with excitement, not for a single competitor but for both. "Thomas! Mari! Thomas! Mari!" The chants echoed through the arena as the audience surged with energy, eager to witness what Thomas could do and what Mari would unleash next.

A raised hand signaled the beginning. No words were spoken, and no rules were recited. Just a swift motion and the battle began.

Simultaneously, Thomas and Mari unleashed blasts of aura. Swirling colors collided midair, sending ripples of force across the stadium. Flames erupted, only to be swallowed by shimmering portals. Fists flew. The atmosphere was electric, chaotic, and relentless.

The spectators never sat down. Every move brought a fresh wave of cheers. Mari began darting through portals with increasing speed, fists and kicks flying as she attacked from every angle. Thomas countered, raising his arms to block and deflect each strike. Then, his aura surged, an intense, purplish glow radiating from him like wildfire.

Mari inhaled deeply and slammed her fists together. Portals flared into existence above, below, beside him, surrounding Thomas. She dashed into one and began accelerating, firing through them like a cannonball from every direction.

Thomas, eyes darting, planted an aura at each portal's entrance. Every time she emerged left, right, up, or down, his skin prickled with anticipation. He ducked, twisted, blocked a dance of survival and instinct.

Suddenly, he clapped his hands together. A cold wave of icy-blue aura surged outward, wrapping around the portals and freezing them solid. Mari had only a split second to escape, diving out of the first portal just in time.

The ice shattered.

Thomas lunged forward, fist flying.

Mari spun in midair, her foot arcing toward him.

The two blows connected simultaneously, his fist to her face, her kick to his jaw.

They crashed to the ground in tandem, gasping for breath.

A pause.

Then, "TIE!"

The word boomed through the speakers, triggering an eruption from the crowd. There were cheers, claps, foot-stomping, and students leaping into the air. It was pandemonium.

From the stands, Elias and Eva cheered the entire time. When Eva called out for Thomas, Elias shouted for Mari. Then they switched. To them, the battle was thrilling, not threatening. And now, as the match ended, they clapped wildly, excitement radiating from every part of them. The surrounding students were just as thrilled.

As the adrenaline began to fade, the energy across the stadium softened. The crowd buzzed with laughter, chatter, and high-fives. Thomas and Mari were given just enough time to get their injuries treated before they were called back to the center of the field.

Applause still echoed through the arena.

A voice rang out over the speakers:

"Coming in at a tie and claiming first place together, MARI AND THOMAS!"

The crowd erupted again, stomping, cheering, and shouting both names in unison.

Thomas grabbed Mari's hand and raised it high. They beamed. They'd made it.

Thomas had unlocked his aura.

But more importantly?

He was finally finishing the school year like a normal student.

26

THE WORLD IS WATCHING

It had been a full week since the tournament, and Thomas and Mari had become two of the most talked-about students in school. Everywhere they went, they were greeted with high fives, nods, and even acknowledgment from teachers. For Mari, this was nothing new. But for Thomas, it was like stepping into an entirely different world.

Brody, meanwhile, remained a little distant. He had known the truth all along. Every day, he watched the school gates, his thoughts returning to the mysterious handprint he had seen. He couldn't shake the feeling that there was more to it than anyone realized. Silas stayed close by, offering steady support, trying to help Brody feel strong in the aftermath of his tournament loss.

Elias and Thomas were finally settling into a sense of nor-malcy. Decay hadn't appeared in weeks, and both boys were finally sleeping better. Thomas had started using his aura in everyday life; it felt natural now, like an extension of himself. Even the teachers began to treat him differently. Some apologized, expressing guilt for disregarding what he had endured.

Mari and Eva went about their daily routines with little trouble from the usual bullies. But Mari began to notice something troubling: without Thomas serving as the school's emotional punching bag, other students were starting to get targeted. Eva, however, didn't seem to notice. She still talked about Thomas at least once or twice a day, convinced that everything was back to normal and that everyone was happy.

Far from the classrooms, deep beneath the school, a dimly lit room waited in silence. Four chairs surrounded a long rectangular table. Two men entered the dungeon-like space, their footsteps echoing off the dripping pipes and flickering lights. They stood facing one another. Shadows swallowed their faces. A long silence passed before the man on the left finally spoke.

"I assume something caught your interest?"

"It did."

"The boy?"

"No. The girl."

"Fascinating. So we're not after the same one."

"Seems that way."

"I guess this means the war continues."

"Seems so."

The sound of dripping water echoed again. Then silence, no trace of anyone entering or leaving.

Elsewhere, in the principal's office, a similar conversation was taking place.

Castel stood motionless, his eyes drifting away from Principal Magnus and toward odds and ends around the office, a few knickknacks and a couple of old stuffed animals. Magnus's voice cut through the quiet, gentle but serious.

"Castel, you noticed the VIP boxes were full today."

Castel finally looked at him and sat down. Magnus was already seated, hands clasped on the desk, watching him carefully.

"Yes," Castel said. "I registered their presence. It seems the whole world is watching Thomas and Mari now."

"That's not necessarily a good thing."

"No, Magnus. It's a great thing."

"How?"

"Because now... the real story begins."

27

CELL PHONE

The end of the school year arrived quickly. With all the excitement over the past month, time had flown by. Thomas aced his finals, his aura had practically guaranteed perfect scores. Mari and Elias weren't far behind, both performing at the top of their classes as well. In the middle of the pack were Eva and Silas, both bright, but neither showcased much aura ability when it mattered. Then there was Brody. He passed, but just barely. He had been distracted and broken, and he hated how hollow that made him feel.

Silas knew something was wrong, but Brody kept the truth hidden from everyone else. His stomach had been in knots for weeks, but as the month came to a close, he started to let go. He accepted it. This was how things had turned out, and he'd just have to try harder next year.

Out in the school courtyard, Thomas strolled beneath the late spring sun. Some students clapped him on the back, high-fived him, or stopped to talk. A few thanked him for helping them with aura control; others asked if he'd be around over the summer. Thomas usually played it cool, either shrugging and saying, "Maybe next year," or offering a casual "Nah, busy summer ahead."

Elias and Thomas had already made plans to keep in touch using portals over the break. Elias had embraced his orphan status without shame and offered to visit regardless. Thomas had learned to accept Elias's charmed lifestyle and that his parents used their aura for personal gain. Still, Elias would come to visit, no matter what.

Around them, students wheeled suitcases and balanced boxes as they headed toward the portal pad, the same one they'd arrived on what felt like a lifetime ago.

Thomas pushed open the dormitory's main doors and froze. Brody, Silas, Eva, and Mari stood in the foyer, beaming and waving at him. He blinked in confusion until Elias nudged him with an elbow.

"They're letting everyone into the dorms to say goodbye," Elias said casually. "Loosening the rules now that it's the end."

It made sense. No reason to enforce strict boundaries when students were already packing up.

As Thomas approached the group, they exchanged a knowing look.

"HAPPY BIRTHDAY!" Eva shouted suddenly, accidentally jumping the gun as she fired off a confetti cannon.

Everyone else followed a beat later, yelling the same and launching their cannons in a delayed chorus.

Thomas blinked, startled. "How did you guys even know?"

Elias just smirked. "I have my ways."

Laughter followed as the group moved in for hugs. Thomas embraced each of them, his face softening with an emotion he hadn't felt in a long time belonging. This was the first real birthday celebration he'd had in years. Usually, it was just him and Samuel sneaking a slice of pizza and wandering through the park.

But now he had real friends.

Then came the gift. One by one, each of them pulled out a box, neatly wrapped and labeled with his name. Thomas felt his throat tighten. He swallowed a breath, smiled, and slowly reached for the nearest one.

Tearing through the paper, he froze.

"It's a cell phone," he said, voice cracking slightly.

"We wanted you to keep in touch over the summer," Eva said, cheeks dusted pink.

"I'm not portaling over just to see you every day," Mari teased.

"Yeah! Me and Silas will send you videos," Brody added with a grin.

Elias remained quiet, but he didn't need to say anything. Their plans were already in motion.

Thomas browsed through the phone, noting all the numbers already saved. Even Castel's was in there.

"Where's Castel?" he asked, glancing up.

"Haven't seen him all week," Mari replied with a shrug. "Maybe finals and life caught up to him."

Thomas nodded and smiled faintly, hugging them all again.

They shared cake, downloaded games, and goofed around for a while. But slowly, one by one, the group began to leave until only Thomas remained. The sun dipped low, casting orange light across the courtyard. He sat on his suitcase near the entrance, steeling himself to go.

Then, the dorm doors creaked open.

Castel stepped through. "Good, I didn't miss you."

Thomas looked up. "Still here. Thanks for the number," he said, smiling.

"Of course, man," Castel replied, sitting beside him. "I just wanted to say I'm proud of you. I knew you had it in you."

"Im not that special."

"To get through this year without aura?" Castel shook his head. "It's more than special."

"Stop," Thomas chuckled. "You're making me blush."

Castel laughed and clapped a hand on Thomas's shoulder. "I'll walk you to the portal."

Thomas nodded. Together, they began walking, talking, and smiling as two friends in quiet understanding. As they neared the portal pad, Thomas showed off some of his hybrid magic, already growing more confident with it.

The orphanage awaited him for the summer. But this time, he wasn't returning with uncertainty or dread.

This time, he knew exactly where he belonged and where he'd be next year.

Fin.

* 9 7 9 8 9 9 8 9 2 7 2 0 1 *